LOVE'S DECEPTION

DISCARD

LOVE'S DECEPTION

ADRIANNE BYRD

ARABESQUE®

Recycling programs
for this product may
not exist in your area.

LOVE'S DECEPTION

An Arabesque novel published by Kimani Press/April 2010

First published by BET Publications, LLC in 2000

ISBN-13: 978-0-373-83181-4

© 2000 by Adrianne Byrd

www.kimanipress.com

Printed in U.S.A.

To Alda Townsend.
Here's to new friendships.

Chapter 1

Sitting on top of the world—what a joke.

C. J. Cartel's cold and jaded gaze skittered across downtown Atlanta's cityscape while bitterness rose and left a vile taste in her mouth. The perfect view was just one of the rewards of being CEO of a Fortune 500 company. She took a deep breath and turned from the wall-length window, unimpressed.

She moved across the office with quick, determined strides—her mind already cluttered with the day's agenda. For the most part, C. J. Cartel was nothing more than a name scrolled across important documents, but it was a name with power and influence.

Returning to her desk, she buzzed her secretary.

"Liz, do you have my calendar?" Her tone was hard, quick and to the point—as usual.

"Yes, ma'am," Liz practically sang over the intercom. "I'll bring it in for you."

Seconds later, Liz sauntered through the door, wearing a short tailored suit. Her honey-brown complexion seemed luminous beneath the room's lighting, while each spiral curl crowning her flawless face behaved.

"Here you are," she said with a smile.

C.J. suppressed a scowl. No one had a right to be that perky. "Thanks," she said with a dismissive nod.

Liz didn't move.

Lifting her head, C.J. arched a quizzical brow. "Yes?"

Her secretary's smile brightened as she pulled out a small box. "I got you something." She placed the ivory-papered gift, complete with a bright red bow, in the center of her desk. "Happy birthday!"

Instead of being flattered, C.J. was annoyed. "You shouldn't have."

"Oh, it was no problem." Liz waved off the sarcastic reply with a sweep of her hand. "I know you don't like celebrating your birthday, but when I saw this, I simply couldn't resist."

It was the same excuse she'd used for the past four years, but C.J. swallowed the sharp retort that crested her lips and opened the box. At first sight of the snowball, her breath hitched in her throat and an unexpected emotion nearly paralyzed her.

"Well, take it out of the box."

She obeyed without much thought.

Liz reached over and shook the small orb, and glitter swirled around a beautifully posed ballerina who bore an uncanny resemblance to C.J. "Do you like it?"

She hated it. "I have a lot of work to do, Liz. And so do you." She caught the flicker of disappointment across the secretary's face, but ignored it.

"Yes, ma'am." Liz lowered the gift onto the desk and turned to leave.

C.J. waited until she heard the click of the door before chancing a look, then gave herself a mental kick. She hadn't handled that well at all. Her gaze returned to the gift.

Her birthdays always had a way of playing like a Shakespearean tragedy—the measles, a broken arm, a broken engagement and her father's death. She turned away and struggled to hide her emotions behind the steel armor she spent years building.

But no matter what she did, guilt resided permanently with her conscience. To this day, she felt certain that there was something she could have done to save her father.

Her painful memories came to a screeching halt at the sound of an angry male voice outside her door just seconds before it jerked open.

"There you are!" Travis Edwards's gaze raked her.

She jumped to her feet, more out of anger than surprise.

"I'm sorry, Ms. Cartel. He just barged past me," Liz said with wide-eyed disbelief.

C.J. tilted her head in understanding and gave her secretary permission to leave.

With an apologetic frown, Liz closed the door.

Taking a deep, calming breath, C.J. reclaimed her seat, then centered her icy gaze on her intruder.

Travis Edwards slammed his fist against her desk. "Do you think I'm going to stand by and just let you destroy everything I've worked for without putting up a fight?"

Silently, she prepared for the flare-up of dramatics that usually accompanied men's bursts of outrage.

"You have some damn nerve. I may be old, but I'm no fool. This isn't over by a long shot."

"I'm not in the business of destroying anything, Mr. Edwards," she answered humbly with outspread palms. It was a small white lie, but those never hurt anybody. "Now, if you'd just relax and take a look at our proposal—"

"I'm not looking at anything." He wagged his finger as he continued. Steel glittered in his eyes, signaling he was a man accustomed to battles. But unfortunately, he was at war with one of the best in the business.

"I've heard how you do business, Cartel. I know firsthand about the legions of companies you've destroyed, and I don't intend to be next." His gaze swept over the lavish office with growing contempt.

C.J. watched over wire-rimmed glasses and with

cool aloofness at the incensed gentleman. "Well, I'd hoped that we could discuss this like civilized adults. Since we're one member shy for that, I believe this meeting is over," she announced.

Utter loathing covered Travis's face, while a wild look of desperation filled his eyes. "No. I won't allow you to do this to me."

She had heard every possible success story businessmen recited whenever they stared down the barrel of a hostile takeover, and they all bored her. "This is all very touching, but like I said, this meeting is over."

"Why you b—"

"Watch it, Mr. Edwards. If I were you, I wouldn't say something I'd regret." Her icy tone silenced him without raising a decibel. "Now, the proposal I'm offering doesn't exactly leave you destitute. You'll still be considered a rich man. Isn't that all that really matters?"

"Hell no!" He brushed a hand along his handsomely groomed salt-and-pepper hair. "You think I don't know that Colin Hunter is behind all of this?"

"That's not true." She lied again, but shrugged the guilt off as being a nuisance. What difference did it make if her new vice president initiated the deal?

"I wasn't born yesterday."

Leaning back, she studied the emotionally distraught businessman with developing interest. She knew his kind. He thought he could storm into her office and intimidate her, but she had long ago learned the rules of hardball, and she considered herself a champion.

"No, Mr. Edwards, I think you're cornered. I think you have very little choice but to accept my offer." She glanced at her watch. "And unfortunately, you're wasting my time."

Edwards's handsome features darkened. "This is nothing more than a game to you, isn't it? Well, this is my *life*." He thought he saw a twinge of guilt cross Cartel's delicate features, but it quickly vanished. He should have known better. Behind her dark eyes and warm brown complexion lay an armor of pure ice.

His face reddened, yet this time when he opened his mouth, there was no sound.

C.J.'s bored gaze lifted and cautiously turned concerned.

Edwards grasped at his shoulder and seemed to struggle with the mere task of supplying air to his lungs. His eyes darkened with pain.

She sprang from her chair and jabbed a button connecting her to her secretary. "Call an ambulance," she ordered before Liz could answer.

"Right away, Ms. Cartel."

When she raced around the desk, he grabbed her arm in a painful grip. She winced but didn't bother to protest. "Help is on the way, Mr. Edwards. Try to relax."

His grasp tightened as he struggled to talk. "Y-you did this to me."

Chapter 2

Miami, Florida

Nathan Edwards knelt for a better angle of his nude model. Her glorious ink-black curls cascaded past her caramel-colored shoulders while her seductive liquid brown eyes flirted through the camera lens.

Racy Latin music and the merriment of the growing crowd below the studio drifted through the open windows, while two ceiling fans added little to cool the studio's sweltering heat. Nathan stood and removed his shirt, frustrated by the way it clung to his moist skin. Without skipping a beat, he resumed working.

"I can't tell you how happy I was when you called." Aria jump-started the conversation.

"My schedule has been crazy lately." He stood to adjust the lighting on a nearby lamp. "But I've been meaning to call."

"Well, that's good to hear."

Nathan shook his head, flattered by the way her gaze roamed his exposed chest. "I meant that in the most professional manner possible," he added.

"I didn't."

Her directness never failed to bring a smile to his lips.

"Besides…" she said as she struck a different pose while he resumed working "…hasn't anyone ever told you that all work and no play isn't good for you?"

"I believe you did the last time we worked together."

"You should listen to me." Her fingers circled an erect nipple. "I have just the thing in mind to help you relax."

Nathan frowned. "Aria," he said with a note of warning.

"Yes?" Her gaze feigned innocence and met his bold one.

"Behave."

"I'd rather not."

"That much is obvious." He stopped. "I'd really like to get these done in one session."

She dropped her hands to her hips. "If I didn't know any better, I'd think you were gay."

A low rumble of laughter shook his chest. "Just because I won't give into your…charms?"

"No man has ever refused me before," she stated matter-of-factly. "I mean, you're not even tempted."

Nathan caught the hint, then nodded with a growing smile. Her pride was at stake. "Who said I wasn't tempted?"

Her chin lifted and the damage had been repaired. In truth, Aria was one of his favorite models. His camera loved her, just like any eye that followed the leggy temptress.

As they continued with the shoot, he imagined being lost in the folds of her luscious curves and threading his fingers through her hair. He watched as she ran her tongue across her parted lips, and he struggled to quell his growing desire when her eyes darkened with something akin to passion.

How long had it been since his split with India— nine months? Hell, it seemed like a lifetime.

Aria swayed her hips to the beat of the upbeat music. Her lashes lowered and just like that the mood shifted.

Never mixing business with pleasure had always been a hard and fast rule, and now he was in danger of breaking it.

"Why don't we have a little party of our own?" she offered, closing the sparse distance between them. "One of these days," she whispered, "you're going to realize that you need people."

She struck a nerve, and his smile faded and the mood vanished. "I wouldn't bet on it."

Aria's expression turned serious. "I would bet my life on it." She regarded him. "I've often wondered what caused that pain in those beautiful eyes of yours."

"You're imagining things." He returned his concentration to his work, his earlier temptations forgotten.

"I hate to think that an old flame or something has turned you against love," she persisted, undaunted by his mood swings.

"It was definitely an 'or something.'" He laughed. "Women. Who fills your heads with such wild illusions of love, anyway?"

"It's not who—it's what. And the answer is our hearts. You'd be a lot better off if you'd listen to yours every once in a while, instead of trying to convince yourself that you don't have one."

Silence trailed her final comment.

Nathan weighed her words and even felt there may have been a little truth to them, but he couldn't help how he felt. Love and commitment may be what the rest of the world searched for, but it wasn't for him.

She retrieved her silk robe, her face flushed with anger as she stormed off.

"Where are you going?"

"I'm taking a break," she said over her shoulder.

"What the hell did I do now?"

The slam of the bathroom door was her only answer. He mumbled a curse and struggled not to throw something. "Women. You never know what's going to set them off." And this time he was at a complete loss.

At times like these, he preferred assignments with animals. He glanced at his watch and weighed his options. There were no windows in the bathroom, and he suspected it was simply a matter of time before the humidity forced her out. Or he could just call it a wrap.

He'd given her until the count of ten, and had only reached five before the door opened.

"I'm not angry at you," she said, leaning against the door frame. "Just men like you."

"Well, that clears it up for me."

She shrugged off his sarcasm and tightened her robe's belt. "I mean it. You live the life of a Bohemian, never staying in one place or with one woman for long."

Nathan's brows furrowed at the direction of the conversation.

"It's almost as if you were afraid of committing to anything."

"Or anyone?" he added for her. Her nod completed his puzzle.

A high-pitched voice startled them. He turned toward the studio door to see his assistant, Gina, rushing toward them.

"I need to talk to you." The older woman's tone held a note of urgency.

His situation with Aria needed to be handled with delicacy. "Can you give me a few minutes?" he asked Gina.

"This can't wait. It's about your father."

* * *

Red and white flashing lights blinded fourteen-year-old Carissa. Within seconds, the paramedics brushed her aside in order to tend to her fallen father.

He's not going to make it.

Her heart didn't want to believe her mind's prediction, but the thought held a ring of certainty. Numb, she watched the flurry of activity. He wouldn't leave her. He'd promised.

When they lifted him onto the gurney, she didn't recognize him. His skin was so pale—almost lifeless. Carissa lifted her chin and refused to say goodbye.

He was going to be fine. The words were hollow. Her lungs burned as she slowly became aware that she was holding her breath. She drew in the night's cool air and cleared her head. The doors to the ambulance closed and reality settled and shattered her heart. She would never see him again…

Carissa shook away the memory, but still felt like that scared fourteen-year-old as guilt seeped through her every pore. No matter how hard she tried, she couldn't block the image of Travis Edwards's accusing gaze or words. In her mind, his dark eyes resembled her father's.

Standing alone in a crowded E.R., she'd finally come full circle. Her stomach twisted into knots. This was the last place she thought she'd ever end up.

A nurse appeared and asked a stream of unanswerable questions. Seconds later, the E.R.'s whirlwind of activity had dulled to a slower pace, but not the thoughts inside her head.

A sudden wave of nausea caught her off guard and sent her rushing to find the nearest restroom. Her entire body trembled as fear blended with tears.

"It's not my fault," she recited in a low whisper when she finally came up for air. But no matter how many times she said the words, she couldn't bring herself to believe them.

She didn't know how long she sat there hugging the cold porcelain. If she could have her way, she would have remained huddled against it forever.

Stop your whimpering and get up. She recognized the harsh voice inside her head as her father's. He hated weakness, and he always seemed to find that flaw in her. The command echoed in her head again, and she stood.

Shakily, she wiped the tears from her eyes, then managed to straighten her clothes. She stepped from behind the stall door with her chin forced high. At the sink, she splashed cold water on her face.

"Ms. Cartel?" Liz poked her head inside the restroom.

Her solitude invaded, C.J. stole another glance at herself, disgusted with the image that stared back. Her long wavy curls lay haphazardly to one side, what little makeup she wore was all but gone, and her clothes were rumpled despite the earlier straightening.

"Are you all right?" Liz moved in farther, her eyes wide with shock.

"Of course. I just came in here to get away from that madhouse out there." She cringed at the lie.

Liz's expression told her she didn't believe her, but she wisely chose to change the subject. "It took some time, but I was finally able to locate a relative. Seems Mr. Edwards doesn't have much family."

"Why didn't you let someone at his company do all that?" C.J. worked to pull her thick hair back into a tight bun at the nape of her neck.

"Would you believe that they were as much at a loss as I was on who to contact? Finally, someone remembered that Edwards has a son. But after all that digging, I have a feeling he didn't want to be found."

"Is he on his way?"

"Now *that's* the million-dollar question. Let's just say Nathan Edwards didn't seem too choked up over the news."

Chapter 3

Colin Hunter received the news of Travis Edwards's heart attack with a twinge of surprise and guilt. But by the time he hung up the phone, a slow smile creased his lips. He eased back in his chair, stretched his arms behind his head, and filled his lungs with a deep cleansing breath.

As he looked around the room, he wished he could make a toast with someone. Victory never smelled nor tasted so sweet. He was in his mid-fifties, but he swore he had the energy of a thirty-year-old. Hell, he wanted to do more than celebrate. He wanted to send C. J. Cartel a wreath of roses.

"You gotta love that woman," he boasted aloud, then slithered to his feet and headed to the bar. He'd spent the past five years trying to put Edwards out of business when all he had really had to do was win Cartel over.

He shook his head as he poured himself a drink. There was still a lot about the cold businesswoman that remained a mystery to him. Like what drove her so hard and why did she spend so much time trying to prevent anyone from getting too close?

Colin dismissed the intriguing questions with a casual shrug. Who cared? The only thing that mattered was that he had succeeded in destroying Travis Edwards's precious company.

Carissa paced the E.R. and worried over what took the doctors so long. Guilt and regret narrated the scene in her office as it replayed in her head. She was too harsh, her motive too selfish. She'd finally become the son her father had always wanted. And she was ashamed of herself.

Liz had left to take care of her five-year-old son, and to Carissa's utter amazement, no one from Edwards Electronics had come to visit its president. She remembered the stories she'd heard about Travis Edwards and, in fact, had dismissed them. She'd learned a long time ago never to place her trust in rumors—especially since there were just as many circulating about her.

She wondered if there was any truth to them. If there were, Travis Edwards and her father would have been great friends. *Where is his son? He should have been here by now.*

As time ticked on, she concluded that he wasn't coming. Just as she hadn't.

Another wave of shame washed over her. She was drowning in her own sea of emotional torment. So why was she staying? She didn't know this man. Travis's accusation echoed in her ears, and she pressed her eyelids shut. *Please, God, say it's not my fault.*

Her weak words lacked conviction and she stopped pacing and dropped her weight into a nearby chair. "Happy birthday," she mumbled under her breath.

"Ms. Cartel?"

She stood with expectant eyes as a distinguished-looking African-American doctor approached. "Please don't let it be bad news," she whispered in prayer. Her heart inched up into her throat when she was unable to read the man's expression.

"Yes. I'm Dr. Peterson and I'll be your fiancé's physician. I was wondering if I could ask you a few questions."

Her mouth opened, but no words came out. She should tell the doctor the truth, but if she did that, the hospital wouldn't keep her abreast of what was happening. Besides, what harm could come of her masquerading as the man's fiancée?

Nathan left Atlanta's Hartsfield Airport and paid little attention to the exit signs along the highway. When he'd jumped into the rental car two hours ago, he'd had every intention of driving to Northside

Hospital—but somewhere along the way, he'd lost his nerve. Going to see his father would be against everything he stood for and would break the promise he'd made to himself…and to his mother.

Why should he go? The man had abandoned them. Nathan still remembered the heartbreak when his mother told him his father wasn't coming back, but most of all, he remembered his mother's tears. A low curse resonated in his chest.

Rage and bitterness erupted within Nathan as he gripped the steering wheel. He couldn't put the past behind him when years of heartache blazed within him.

For the fifth time that evening, Nathan passed the exit for the hospital. *Damn Travis Edwards to hell.*

Liz pushed open her grandmother's bedroom door, again disturbed by the older woman's eerie stillness. It amazed her at how long she'd sit and gaze out the window at nothing—like she was waiting for something or someone.

Goose bumps pimpled Liz's skin at the sudden drop in temperature as she eased into the room. She never could understand why Nana preferred the room so cold.

Liz moved closer. "How was your day, Nana?" she inquired, neither expecting nor receiving an answer.

Funny, she thought, at how irony had a strange way of lacing its fingers throughout one's life. She stroked her grandmother's soft silvery hair and hummed an old tune.

A soft, thin sigh escaped Nana's lips as she tilted up her chin.

Liz smiled and wondered whether she'd recognized the song. Inhaling, she drew in an odd combination of baby powder and Ben Gay. *I'm going to miss this time with you.* The words floated across her head and a rush of tears slid from her eyes.

Nurse Anne Browning smiled at Carissa as she explained the visiting hours. "We normally don't allow non-family members in the ICU, but Dr. Peterson has made an exception in your case being that you're Mr. Edwards's fiancée. You're more than welcome to stay as long as you'd like. But we do ask that you leave during shift changes between seven and nine."

"Thank you," Carissa said, avoiding eye contact. She turned and slid open the glass door and eased her head inside Travis's small quarters. Her hackles stood at attention as her gaze centered on the body lying so still. The steady beep from the monitor overhead added relief to her troubled heart.

Taking a deep breath, she once again tried to reassure herself that he'd pull through. He had to. She simply couldn't handle another death on her conscience. Instead of leaving, she moved farther into the room as if pulled by some invisible force.

As she drew near, she was struck by the uncanny resemblance Edwards had to her father. Soon, she found herself studying him. From the strong angles of his face to the broad frame of his athletic body, his appearance nearly convinced her that her eyes were playing tricks on her.

She reached for his hand. It was cold. She blinked and swallowed the lump in her throat. Why hadn't she come when her father had asked for her?

A chill raced along her spine. She shivered. Hospitals were always cold, she thought bitterly. Another reason why she hated them.

A chair sat a few feet from the bed and she contemplated staying a few minutes longer. Really, it didn't make any sense for her to stay. In truth, she'd done more than what was expected.

She pulled up the chair and sat. But as words of apology cluttered her head, she could do no more than hold the older man's hand and allow her tears to fall.

Early the next morning, Nathan stood outside the ICU with anxiety twisting knots in his stomach. His nervousness surprised him and accelerated his heartbeat.

With his jaws clenched, Nathan's heart hardened as bitter memories monopolized his thoughts. Why in the hell had he come here? He turned from the door while a war with his emotions raged on, but something stopped him from leaving.

Just get it over with.

It sounded like a simple command, but he'd be damned if he could do it. However, the urge to see the giant of his childhood, helpless, forced him to act.

The unit was cold, despite the morning sunlight streaming through the windows.

"May I help you?"

Nathan turned toward kind, inquisitive eyes. "Yes, I'm here to see my father, Travis Edwards."

"Yes, of course." She looked down at her watch. "You have a few minutes before the shift change if you want to see him. I don't know whether his fiancée is with him. If you'd follow me, he's at the last unit by the window—"

"I think I can find it." He managed to maintain an amicable smile, then headed off in the pointed direction.

He pulled back the sliding curtain and his gaze swept across his father's still face. Another jolt of anger struck him. The years had been kind. Travis Edwards's appearance hadn't changed in thirty years.

"I shouldn't have come," Nathan declared in a low voice.

A soft moan startled him. He blinked when a woman lifted her head from the bed.

He watched, fascinated, as waves of dark curls spilled back from the woman's head to reveal her flawless features. The woman's natural beauty astonished him. She stretched languorously, then stifled a yawn behind her hand, still unaware of his presence.

However, all illusions of love at first sight vanished when she reached for his father's hand before opening her eyes.

Jealousy eclipsed Nathan's adoration and his greeting was sharp and spiteful. "You must be my father's latest conquest."

Chapter 4

Anger boiled through Carissa's veins as her eyes narrowed to thin slits. "Just where in the hell do you get off?" She rose to her feet.

A single brow lifted on the man's otherwise unchanged expression.

Contemptuously, her gaze raked the tall stranger. But her disdain didn't last. The man's handsome dark features caught her off guard. His muscular physique appeared to be the result of hours in the gym. With skin the color of roasted chestnuts and eyes the color of dark chocolate, she was mesmerized by what could only be called perfection.

She forced herself to blink and break the trance. It

was then that she became aware of his reserved apprai-sal, too.

Her anger renewed itself. "I believe I asked you a question."

She watched a muscle twitch along his temple, and his eyes darkened. Even though she'd been in countless confrontations, her stomach twisted into knots beneath his hard glare. She steeled herself for a verbal attack.

Instead, the brewing storm in his eyes calmed suddenly and he turned toward the still body lying between them. "I'm sorry. That was uncalled-for."

The rich timbre of his voice, which she could've sworn wasn't there seconds ago, weakened her knees and had her draw in a quick breath just to clear her head and abate her own anger.

She followed his somber gaze, and his sudden ten-derness touched her. Realizing it was time to leave, she turned and reached for her purse. "I'll leave you two alone." She headed toward the door when her conscience forced her to turn back, but all thoughts of an apology vanished the moment their eyes met.

The gentleness she'd witnessed seconds ago had vanished. In its place a hard and unforgiving expres-sion stared back at her. The man was a jumbled bag of contradictions, she concluded. Frustrated, Carissa clamped her jaws shut, then turned to leave.

Nathan's curious gaze followed her, then lowered back toward the bed. His hands clenched at his sides as he waited for remorse or even regret to assault him, but instead he felt…well, he wasn't quite sure what he felt.

Despite the uncanny resemblance, Nathan continued to stare at a stranger. For so long he'd dreamed of this day—the day when he'd have the opportunity to confront the man who had destroyed his childhood and killed his mother. No, Travis Edwards didn't pour an overdose of sleeping pills down his mother's throat, but Nathan still considered him responsible.

So why are you here?

He didn't know. A list of possibilities had run through his head in the car: responsibility, vengeance, peace. None of them made any sense. He closed his eyes and struggled to pull himself together. In his mind, all he saw was a picture of his mother. What would she think of his being here?

With a heavy heart, he drew in a deep breath and physically ached when her image faded.

Nathan blinked his eyes dry. "I wish I knew where to begin." He exhaled and struggled to lift the weight of the world from his shoulders. "I spent so much time hating you—most of my life, in fact. Even now, there's a part of me that wants some type of revenge for the *years* of pain we endured."

He shook his head and added, "But it's too late for that now. It's too late for a lot of things." Tears obscured his vision as his emotions overwhelmed him. "I just wish I could understand. Or at least know what went wrong. Maybe I'll never know." He laughed at himself. "Hell, I'm a grown man. I have no business believing in fairy tales. Who am I trying to kid? We were never happy, were we?" He looked at his father's face, almost searching for a confirmation.

Jabbing his clenched hands into his pants pockets, he tried to finish. "I guess it's pretty customary for family to try to reach some type of closure at times like these. The truth is, I sort of feel like a hypocrite for coming here. But I had to. I need some kind of peace so I can move on." Lowering his head, he wished the floor would swallow him whole. "I just want to know *why* you left."

Of course, he didn't really expect an answer, but the room's silence disappointed him all the same. "I have to get out of here." Before the tears that crested his eyes fell, Nathan rushed from the room.

Carissa sat defeated behind the wheel of her car with her head slumped against the headrest. She would rise above this, she assured herself. This whole mess wasn't her problem. How was she to know the man had medical problems?

She pinched the bridge of her nose while her thoughts drifted to Edwards's son and the familiar mixture of pain and anger in his eyes. They were emotions she knew all too well.

Eighteen years had passed since her father's death—a long time to live with regret. Had she been a better daughter, things may have turned out differently, she reasoned.

Carl James Cartel had been a hard and ruthless businessman and was equally hard on his loved ones, if one could call barking orders and ruling every inch of his family's lives love. As a teenager, Carissa didn't think so, but as an adult, she held a different view.

A plane crash had claimed her mother when Carissa was a toddler, leaving her alone with her father. It took until adolescence before Carissa became a rebel without a cause, and the true battle of the wills alienated father and daughter.

An endless supply of anger had been stored in her hormonally imbalanced body, and every prank and act of disobedience was meant to punish her father for reasons that now escaped her. Her outlandish conduct never stopped, even after she was slammed into a private Catholic school. And they weren't even Catholic.

A sad laugh escaped her as she shook away her reverie. She had more than made up for those lost days. Since his death, she'd made sure she attended the schools he'd outlined, and she had joined her uncle Charles in the family business, then even went on to run the company after his death as well.

Now, she couldn't remember the person she'd been or the dancer she'd dreamed of becoming. Guilt drove her to become the person her father wanted. Somewhere along the line, his dreams became her goals and the real Carissa had ceased to exist.

For years, she'd heard people refer to her as cold and calculating—a progeny of her old man. And it was true. She'd built a career by lying and manipulating her way to the top. Tears slid from her eyes. Somehow, somewhere, she'd sold her soul for forgiveness from her father and she hated herself for it.

Was it too late to change?

During the drive home, her thoughts scattered in numerous directions, then ended in a severe migraine. She needed a vacation, she concluded, then laughed at the outrageous thought. What would she *do* on a vacation but go crazy? The concept of having nothing to do was enough to cause the fine hairs on the back of her neck to stand at attention.

She arrived at her penthouse in the center of Buckhead. The promise of a hot shower awaited her upstairs. After that, she'd steal a couple of hours of sleep.

Staying busy would allow her to forget the past twenty-four hours. And that was exactly what she wanted to do—forget.

Relief flooded her the moment her key slid into the lock. She didn't get far into the apartment before kicking off her shoes and singing, "Home sweet home."

Next, she peeled her clothes off one layer at a time and formed a trail of material leading all the way to her bathroom door. Shortly after, a hard steady stream of hot water erased every residue of stress.

Behind closed lids, Nathan Edwards's dark, sinful eyes with an odd mixture of pain stared back at her. Maybe there was something she could do to help him through this horrible time. Her eyes flew open. What in the hell was wrong with her? Yesterday, she was out conquering the world, and today she was trying to win a Good Samaritan badge for her old Girl Scout troop.

She stepped from the shower, wrapped a towel around herself, and mumbled a low curse at the initial cool breeze wafting from the air conditioner. But before she could head back into the bedroom, a sharp knock drew her attention to the front door.

Carissa retrieved a robe and raced toward the door. But when she glanced out the peephole, she gasped aloud. "I don't believe it." She flung the door open and rushed to embrace the elegantly dressed woman on the other side. "Aunt Helena. What are you doing here?"

"I came to visit my one and only niece for her birthday. I'm sorry I'm a day late, but my flight was canceled yesterday and I got here as soon as I could." Helena pulled Carissa back at arm's length and took a good look at her. "I swear you grow more beautiful every day," she declared with a broad smile.

Despite herself, Carissa blushed. "Thank you."

"A lot it does for you. When are you going to snare a husband and give me some babies to spoil?"

Carissa pretended to glance at a watch. "Well, look at that. It took you less than two minutes to jump on my case. That has to be a new record for you."

Helena simply shrugged and smiled.

"You look good, as always," Carissa complimented.

As was her habit, Helena pinched her niece's cheek. "You always did have a good eye." She sighed. "Well, aren't you going to invite me in?"

"I'm sorry. Come in." She gestured with a sweep of her hand and assisted with the luggage. "I take it that you're going to be staying a while?"

"Just for a few weeks. I knew I couldn't depend on you to find time for me in your busy schedule to conquer the world. So I took matters into my own hands and here I am. And you can just forget about trying to get rid of me."

"I wouldn't dream of it," Carissa said with a genuine smile, then escorted her aunt to the guest room.

"I absolutely love what you've done with this place. Let me guess, you went with Lars for the decor, am I right?"

"You always say to go with the best."

Her aunt's eyes widened. "I must write this historical moment down. Carissa Jeanette Cartel heeds my advice. Will the world's wonders never cease?"

"Very funny."

She pinched Carissa's cheeks again, eliciting yet another frown. "I was so surprised when Liz told me you weren't at work. I actually harbored hopes of you stashing some gorgeous hunk in here and having your way with him, but then I realized how unlikely that scenario was—so I rushed right over to see if perhaps the kidnappers left a ransom note."

"You know I do occasionally take time off."

Her aunt's delicate brows arched.

"What?"

"Don't forget who you're talking to. Something must be dreadfully wrong for you to still be in your robe this late in the morning with large duffel bags under your eyes. Have you been crying?"

"Does nothing ever get by you?" Carissa asked, shaking her head.

"Rarely." She sat on the king-size bed and patted the vacant spot beside her. "Now, sit right here and tell me what's bothering you, sweetheart."

Carissa loved her feisty yet nosy aunt and, being honest with herself, she realized she was glad she'd come. Obediently, she sat down. "To be honest with you, Auntie, I think I've finally done it. I have finally made a complete mess of my life. And right now I don't know what to do about it."

"Sounds serious." Helena frowned. "Maybe you should start from the beginning. I tend to get confused when I come in on the tail end of things."

"The beginning?" Carissa shook her head. "You already know the beginning. It started when I made the foolish decision to step into my father's shoes."

"You mean the ones I told you to leave alone?"

"All right, all right. Are you here looking for the chance to say you told me so?"

"Of course I am, dear. I live for these things. I have no children of my own, so I look forward to the time I can prove my superior knowledge to you."

Carissa laughed. "You're too kind."

"I do try to be. And you're being evasive. What happened?"

"I think I may have killed a man."

Silence trailed her sentence, and Carissa had to look up to make sure her aunt hadn't passed out.

Helena shook her head. "A funny thing happens when you hit sixty. Your hearing has a nasty habit of playing tricks on you."

"It's no trick." Carissa exhaled and tried again. "It started quite innocently. Colin Hunter, my new vice president, brought this small electronics company to my attention. I reviewed the statistics. On paper, there wasn't anything that really stood out, but it definitely showed promise. With the right direction, I can see it doing quite well. So we looked into acquiring it. There was just this one minor setback."

"You had to knock someone off?" Helena guessed.

"No." Carissa playfully slapped her aunt's knee.

"Well, hurry up and get to the good part."

"The so-called good part came when the owner refused to sell. It was really no big deal to me, but Hunter persisted."

"Your VP?"

"Yeah. Well, anyway, one thing led to another and we were able to acquire the company anyway. And, as expected, the owner blew his top. But what I didn't expect was for the man to suffer a massive heart attack in my office."

Helena's eyes rounded with astonishment. "What did you do?"

"Everything happened so fast. I got Liz to call 911 while I stayed with the guy until help arrived, then I went with him to the hospital."

"Oh, my goodness. Is he all right?"

"No. During surgery he suffered a stroke and slipped into a coma."

Carissa waited for her aunt to say something, but when she didn't respond, she looked up at Helena's blank expression.

"Please tell me you're joking," Helena said.

"I wish I was. But believe it or not, it gets worse."

"He didn't—"

"No," Carissa cut her off. "He's still in a coma. However, I had to lie to the staff and pose as this man's fiancée in order to see him."

"Well, that's completely understandable. I would have done the same thing."

Carissa held up her hand. "There's more."

Helena eyed her suspiciously. "What?"

"The man's estranged son shows up." Carissa stood and paced the floor. "I couldn't bring myself to tell him what really happened. In fact, our meeting turned out to be downright hostile. He was rude and the next thing I know I'm practically snapping the man's head off."

"I see."

Carissa turned to face her. "You do?"

"No, but finish the story."

"That's it. This all happened in the past twenty-four hours. I figured I'd go back to the hospital later today and check on him."

"Which one—the father or the son?"

"The father, of course. I think it's in my best interest to avoid the son. There's something unsettling about him."

Helena's brows shot up. "Really? How's that?"

"I don't know. He seems dark and jaded somehow."

Her aunt crossed her arms. "Sounds to me like you two have a few things in common."

"What do you mean?"

"Dark? Jaded? Have you looked in the mirror lately?"

Carissa rolled her eyes.

"All right. I'll shut up—for now. You've already been through a lot dealing with this situation. So why don't you go and get some rest? You look exhausted. I'll unpack, and when you wake up, I'll have a nice little lunch prepared for us."

"I have to admit that sounds tempting, but I probably should just grab a quick nap and rush on over to the office. I can probably make it in by noon."

"You'll do no such thing. You'll sleep, then pretend to be a gracious hostess and have lunch with your aging aunt."

Carissa opened her mouth.

"And I won't hear another word about it. Now off to bed." Helena waved her away.

"Fine. I give up." Sighing, Carissa headed out of the room, feeling as though she were six years old again.

Helena smiled. "I think this little visit is just what we both needed."

Carissa groaned.

Chapter 5

Nathan wanted to, but he couldn't force himself to leave the hospital. What in the hell was wrong with him? He'd performed his duty as a son, despite being unprepared to fight the ghosts of the past. It was time to return to his life, time to forget what he'd seen here—and what he was feeling.

In his mind's eye, he remembered the last time he'd seen his father. It was days after he'd returned home from Vietnam. Nathan shook his head at his crazy effort to search for a lost father. Was he insane?

But what if he had lost him yesterday? No sooner had the question crossed his mind did he regret asking it. An unexpected rush of tears blurred his vision. "Hell, I never had him," he muttered under his breath.

In the back of his mind, he knew that wasn't true. Throughout his childhood and even as an adult, he'd thought of his father. However, he'd never been able to forgive him.

Nathan found a pay phone, then cursed at his inability to find change in his pockets. Gina's constant nagging for him to purchase a cell phone echoed in his head. Grudgingly, he called the operator to place a collect call.

"I accept," Gina told the operator, then launched a series of questions at her employer. "How are you? Have you seen him yet? Do you need me to come to Atlanta?"

"Fine, yes, and that won't be necessary," he answered, then allowed an awkward moment of silence to elapse.

"I'm a great listener," she suggested.

"That's the reason I called." A much-needed smile lifted the corners of his lips. "I don't know how long I'm going to hang out down here."

"You take as much time as you need. Aria has already called and she completely understands the situation. She wanted me to remind you that she'll be in Atlanta next week for that promotional party."

"I doubt that I'll be here that long."

"I have to admit we were a little bewildered yesterday."

Nathan nodded against the phone. Most people believed his real father had been dead for years. So no doubt his father's miraculous materialization surprised everyone. But he'd deal with that later. "I was wondering if I could ask you a favor?"

"Anything. If you want me to go over and feed George, I've already taken care of it."

He smiled at the thought of his loyal German shepherd. "You're a doll."

"I'm glad you've noticed."

"I know I can always count on you."

"You just deal with your father and call me if you need anything."

"Will do." Nathan hung up, then placed another call. "Hello."

"Guess who happens to be in the neighborhood?"

"Well, I'll be damned, Nate. What are you doing in town?"

"I guess there's no way for you to know this, but Travis is in the hospital." As he expected, a long silence trailed his announcement.

"So you came to see him?" His stepfather's voice lowered.

"I know. I'm not quite sure how I feel about being here, either. Hell, to be honest with you, I'm surprised I came."

"So am I."

Nathan shook his head. What did he expect? A thirty-year-old rivalry still existed between the two men. And without his stepfather actually saying anything, Nathan sensed that his own loyalty was in question.

It was a feud he'd understood at times, then had been completely mystified by at others. However, before the war, the men had actually been the best of friends. *We would have died for one another,* his stepfather had quoted numerous times in the past. But circumstances change, and everyone's lives traveled different roads.

"Are you game for getting together later on?" Nathan asked.

"Would you rather I come there?"

The offer rendered Nathan speechless. "I can't ask you to do that, but thanks anyway."

"Well, I just want you to know that I'm here for you."

Nathan smiled. "Of course. I know that."

"Good." His stepfather's voice perked.

"Back to the reason I called. I thought that since I was going to be in town for a little while that maybe we can get together for dinner or something."

"Well, now, that would be nice. Do you still have that apartment in town?"

"Yeah, lucky for me. Last month I was thinking about selling the place."

"You know you're always welcome to crash here. In fact, it would be a great chance for us to play catch-up. Are you still seeing that anthropologist?"

Nathan rolled his eyes heavenward. "You mean India?"

"Ah, yes. A beautiful name for a beautiful woman."

"Beauty is in the eye of the beholder. We broke up a while back."

"Anything you want to talk about? I know a thing or two about women."

"Is that all, a thing or two?"

"Son, that's all a man can hope to achieve on the subject in one lifetime."

They laughed.

"Nate, how about you call me around three on my cell phone and we'll compare schedules then?"

"Sounds like a plan."

By the time the call ended, Nathan's spirits had lifted.

Hanging up, he exhaled a long, tired sigh and retraced his steps back to the ICU. Once there, his nerves had calmed and a certain type of peace settled within him as he stared down at his father. As he watched, he couldn't help but wonder where his father's mind traveled…

Chicago. April 2, 1966

Captain Travis Edwards of the United States Army rapped on the Plexiglas in the nursery, trying in vain to grab his newborn son's attention. Pride expanded the young officer's chest while he waved and mouthed the words, "Hello, fella."

Nathan returned a lopsided grin, which Travis took as a sign of exceptional intelligence. A world of future possibilities floated in Travis's head.

A heavy hand slapped across his back. "Congratulations, Captain. I see you finally did something right for a change."

Travis shook his head and answered his best friend,

Smokey, without a backward glance. "Jealousy's a bitch, ain't it?"

His friend's boisterous laugh stole another smile from Travis. "I really did do something right this time, didn't I?"

"Yeah. I'd say by the way that li'l guy's beaming at you, you got yourself a fan for life."

"Trust me, buddy. I have no plans on screwing this assignment up."

"Well, good luck to ya. The worst you can do is turn out to be like my old man. Congratulations again. I got to head on over to the club. I'll catch you later?"

"Yeah, sure thing. I'll tell Val you stopped by." Travis continued to watch his son in the nursery, enjoying the strength of the newly formed bond.

For months, he and Val had been preparing for a little girl. They'd even picked out the name Natalie, named after his eccentric grandmother. Now the name had been modified to Nathan. Visions of baseball and football games materialized in Travis's head, and a double dose of testosterone pumped through his veins.

Later, Travis peeked in on his wife and smiled at her sleeping form. "I'm a lucky man," he declared and eased inside the door. She was even more beautiful now than the day he met her.

As if sensing his presence, her eyes fluttered open. "Hi there." She smiled.

He loved her husky vibrato, the gentle curl of her hair and the warmth of her eyes. "Hi there yourself."

He rested a hip against the bed, then leaned down and kissed her.

"Have you seen him?" Pride made her smile wider and even more beautiful.

"Yeah. He's something, ain't he?"

"Isn't he," she corrected playfully. Her few years as an English teacher made correcting everyone's grammar a habit.

"He sure is."

They laughed, then just gazed at each other. A pool of love deepened within their hearts, making words unnecessary to express how they felt.

Travis reached for her hand and kissed her wedding band. "Our little family is growing."

"I think this is the happiest day of my life."

"What about our wedding day?"

"It's a close second."

"I think they both tie for first place." He laughed.

"I love you," she whispered.

"I love you more." He kissed the ring again. "You're going to make a wonderful mother."

"And you're going to make an excellent father."

Chapter 6

Nathan reached into his pocket and pulled out a crumpled piece of paper he'd received from Gina and stared at the name Elizabeth Townsend, administrative assistant of Cartel Enterprises.

From what he understood from Gina, this was the woman who'd called about his father. Nathan contemplated contacting her to find out what happened yesterday. As the thought crossed his mind, a contradicting thought questioned why he even cared.

"I'm going to drive myself crazy with this." He balled the paper back in his fist and swore under his breath. Out of the corner of his eye, he saw a familiar outfit. His mind raced back to the beautiful woman he'd clashed with that morning.

Despite the shame of his earlier behavior, he raced after the figure. When he rounded the corner, he stopped in his tracks. It wasn't her.

He took a calming breath to slow his accelerated heartbeat. A strange reaction, he thought as he turned and went in search of the cafeteria. In retrospect, he had to admit that the woman he'd discovered by his father's side was gorgeous. So much so, he realized his harsh words were more out of jealousy than anger.

When he remembered that the nurse had identified her as his father's fiancée, he shook his head. The woman was too young for Travis.

A few minutes later, Nathan sat relishing his first jolt of caffeine for the day while worrying over Travis's condition. In the back of his mind, he wondered if there was something he should do. Anything would be better than this waiting game.

He warmed to the thought. Maybe he could use this time to learn more about what had happened. He remembered the slip of paper and retrieved it from his pocket. The first place he would try to get some answers would be Cartel Enterprises.

"You murdered my father!" Fire simmered in Nathan Edwards's gaze and burned a hole through Carissa.

She stepped back and mouthed the word no. *The accusation rumbled in her head like a freight train, rendering her powerless against the field of guilt it left in its wake.*

He matched her movement, bearing down on her as if preparing to attack. "I should give you a taste of your own medicine. Maybe you'd like it if I stripped you of everything—robbed you of your dignity. I'd love nothing more than to wipe that 'holier than thou' smirk off that smug face of yours. Maybe afterward, I'd discard you like a piece of trash."

Backed against the wall, she shook her head, still unable to voice any protest.

His head lowered, his hot breath rushed against her face.

"You like playing God, don't you?"

Unshed tears stung her eyes. His anger broke her heart. He had *stripped her—with his words and disgust. She'd never felt this vulnerable—this ashamed.*

"It's only business. It's not personal." She managed to whisper. Tears of remorse crested and splashed over the rims of her eyes.

"It sure as hell doesn't feel *like business."*

Carissa turned her head, drenching the pillow. "No," she cried out, then bolted upright in bed, stunned and disoriented by her surroundings. "Christ," she mumbled and rubbed an open palm across her face. "It was only a dream."

She glanced over at the clock, not surprised that she'd slept well into the afternoon.

Shape up, girl, her father's voice demanded inside her head. She groaned in response.

Jumping out of bed, she rushed to get dressed. A list

of things to do scrolled through her head. When she bolted out of her room, a waft of smoke stung her eyes and the stench of something burning assaulted her nose.

"What in the hell?" She headed toward the kitchen.

"Good, you're finally up," her aunt said with a quick glance over her shoulder. "I hope I didn't wake you up with all of this." She waved her hands frantically trying to dissipate the billowing smoke.

"Why didn't the alarm go off?"

"Oh, that. Well, I always unhook that before I start cooking."

"Cooking? Since when do you cook?" Carissa turned on the fan over the stove.

"Actually, I just started taking lessons six weeks ago. And I've been having a wonderful time. I have this one partner who makes the most wonderful meatballs."

Carissa could only manage to stare at her aunt.

"Well, maybe we can talk about it another time." Helena dusted the flour from her hands, then removed her apron. "I see you're not up to it right now."

Carissa made a sign of the cross before shaking her head.

"Please stop that. You're not Catholic. I swear I don't know why your father sent you to that school."

"To get me out of his hair, if I remember correctly. Come on. Help me get some of these windows open in here before we pass out from smoke inhalation."

"All right. But I don't think it's really that bad."

"Speak for yourself, Auntie." Carissa laughed. "By the way, what on earth made you want to start taking lessons now?"

"Well, to quote my fourth husband, it's never too late to teach an old dog new tricks."

"If you ask me, this seems to be a very dangerous trick."

"That's why I didn't bother to ask you. I probably shouldn't have tried such a complicated dish, but I was trying to impress you."

"What were you trying to make?"

"Meat loaf."

It took everything Carissa had not to laugh, but it didn't help. Her aunt saw straight through her.

"Fine. You'll know the next time I try to do something nice for you."

Carissa pulled her aunt into her embrace and laughed. "You know I'm so happy you're here."

Helena smiled. "Well, of course you are, dear. We're going to have a great time."

"I'm sure we are. But right now I need to run over to the office."

"Why? It's three in the afternoon. The workday is practically over."

"I know. But I'm just going to run over and pick up a few things. I promise I won't stay long."

"Is this a promise from Carissa or from C. J. Cartel?"

"What difference does that make?"

"The difference is C.J. is infamous for going back on his word."

"I object."

"Overruled. If I know anything, I know the reputation of the figure you're trying to emulate."

"What are you talking about? Carissa and C.J. are one and the same."

"Now *I* object. I don't think you've completely sold your soul. But if you have, I'm here to help you get it back."

"My hero." Carissa smiled. "Now I have to go. Are you going to be able to entertain yourself while I'm gone?"

"You're joking, right?"

"Good. I'll call you when I'm on my way back home." She kissed her and rushed to get dressed.

Liz was living a nightmare. The phone continually rang off the hook, while she tried to coordinate her daily duties. She was used to a busy office, but today was ridiculous.

"Cartel Enterprises."

"Yes. I'd like to speak with an Elizabeth Townsend."

Her brows lifted with curiosity at the deep bass vibrating over the line. "This is Ms. Townsend. How can I help you?"

"Actually, I'm not quite sure," he responded soberly. "You called me yesterday. My name is Nathan Edwards."

Liz's grip tightened on the receiver. "Oh, Mr. Edwards. I'm happy you returned my call. When I spoke with your assistant yesterday, I thought—"

"A lot has happened since then."

His voice was layered with such raw emotions, it tugged at Liz's heartstrings. "I'm sorry, Mr. Edwards. I know this is a very hard time for you."

Silence trailed her apology. For an instant, she thought the call had somehow disconnected.

"Thank you," he finally said. "I was wondering if perhaps I could come by your office and talk about what happened yesterday."

Her mouth gaped open. "You want to talk to me?"

"Will that be a problem?"

Wide-eyed, she glanced around the office. "Well, I don't know."

"You don't know?"

"I mean, I guess not." Dread seeped into her veins. She had a bad feeling about this. But what was she supposed to do?

"Good," Nathan exclaimed. "Where is your office located?"

Chapter 7

Liz jumped, then rushed off the phone at C.J.'s sudden appearance in the office. "Good afternoon," she greeted her with an awkward smile. "I was just—"

"Has my four o'clock appointment arrived?" C.J. strode past Liz, unconcerned with explanations.

"Mr. Fisher's secretary called and canceled. They wanted to get on your schedule next week."

"Why the cancellation?"

"A personal matter had come up."

"Then the answer is no. Shield Industries is Mr. Fisher's number one competitor, right?"

Liz nodded and reached for her legal pad.

"Good. Get them on the phone. We'll give them the contract. Any other calls?"

"I placed all your messages on your desk."

"Good." C.J. turned and glided into her office. She was back in her element. Yesterday had to have been a full moon, she reasoned. It was the only explanation for her overly sentimental behavior.

Within minutes, she'd buried herself with teleconferences and paperwork. For the most part, she refused to think about anything dealing with Travis Edwards or his son. It might have been a form of denial, but at least it worked.

Around seven o'clock, Liz poked her head into her office. "Is there anything else I can do for you before I head out?"

C.J. looked around her desk. "Did you ever bring me the profit and loss reports?"

"Dennis called about an hour ago and said that he'll have them finished before noon tomorrow."

She looked up then. "And where is Mr. Duran now?"

"I believe he's gone home for the day."

"Really?" C.J.'s brows arched. "Weren't those reports due yesterday?"

Liz shifted her weight uncomfortably beneath her boss's intense stare. "I would have to check."

Silence filled the space between them, before C.J. spoke. "I can wait."

"Yes, ma'am." Liz disappeared behind the heavy door. In truth, she didn't have to check the calendar and she was certain that C.J. knew that as well. The reports were due yesterday. However, Dennis's wife had fallen ill and he'd enlisted her help to extend the deadline.

Nervously, she returned to C.J.'s office and watched her work for a few seconds before finding her voice. "According to my notes, I—I must have given Dennis the wrong date."

C.J. didn't respond, but kept working.

"I'm sorry. I'm usually good about keeping the dates organized."

Silence.

"Well, if there's nothing else, I should get going." Liz reached to close the door.

"I trust this won't happen again." C.J.'s curt tone sliced the layered tension with precision.

Liz stopped short. "No, ma'am."

"Good night." At the soft click of the door, Carissa looked up. *Fear is respect,* she quoted her father, hoping to burst the bubble of guilt rising in her chest. It worked for a few seconds.

She turned her attention back to her work, but her concentration had been broken. Questions ranging from what she hoped to achieve to whether she liked who she'd become swirled inside her head and made her nauseated. Dropping her elbows onto the desk, she framed her face with her hands and wallowed in self-pity.

Quiet tears trickled down her face and dropped onto the scattered papers on her desk, blurring the ink. The sunset cast peach-colored hues through the open windows. Its fading warmth kissed her and she looked up, almost expecting someone else to be in the room. Standing, she moved toward the window as if under a hypnotic spell and watched a myriad of colors cover the open sky.

The view stole her breath, and something blossomed within. At that moment, she knew it was time for a change.

Liz opened her arms wide and watched with pure unadulterated glee as her five-year-old son jumped into her embrace. "There's my little man." She swung him up into the air as he shrieked with excitement just before a rumble of giggles vibrated his small body.

"Did ya miss me?" she asked, tickling his sides.

"Y-e-e-s-s." He fought for air, but still wanted their game to continue.

"Ms. Townsend?"

Liz shifted her attention to the older woman standing behind her. "Yes?"

A woman's kind cobalt eyes accompanied her wide, genuine smile, before she offered her hand. "My name is Neva St. James. I'm the new head instructor here at the day care. I was wondering if I could take a few minutes of your time?"

"Of course." Liz cast a questioning look down at her son, who hid behind her legs. "Is there something wrong?" she asked, glancing back at Ms. St. James.

"I don't think it's a serious problem. However, I thought you should know that Darius still seems to be having problems playing or participating with the other children."

"Well, he is just shy," Liz explained.

"Yes, ma'am. I see that and I'd hoped that over time this situation would remedy itself. But I think it's getting worse. If it hadn't been for the times when I've seen you with him, I'd swear that your son was a mute. He doesn't say one word from the moment you leave until you come and pick him up. Quite honestly, I'm at my wit's end as to what to do about it."

Liz expelled a long breath. This wasn't the first day care or the first time she'd addressed this issue. "I'll try to have another talk with him."

The teacher smiled. "He really is well-behaved. I was just wondering if perhaps there were something going on at home that could help us better understand what might be troubling him."

"There's nothing wrong with my child's home life," Liz said defensively.

"I'm sorry. I didn't mean to imply that anything's wrong."

"I'll talk with him." She held out her hand and Darius slid his into her grasp.

"Well, please let me know if there's anything I can do to help."

"I'll keep that in mind," Liz said over her shoulder, already heading for the door.

At midnight, Carissa eased behind the steering wheel of her black Lincoln Navigator, bone tired. Accustomed to having the last car left in the parking deck, she'd long ago dismissed the dangers of walking the deck alone. Somewhere in the back of her mind, she'd convinced herself that she could handle anything that came her way.

Savoring the silence, she realized she wasn't ready to go home. Why? There was no one waiting for her. Her aunt had called earlier and said that she'd made plans with some friends. No doubt that meant she'd be out all night.

It's lonely at the top. She emitted a sad laugh, and in the same instant, she wanted to cry. *Damn it!* She punched the steering wheel, then jumped when the horn blared. *Christ.* Her heart thumped hard against her chest. *"What's gotten into me?"* she questioned.

The engine purred to life with a flick of her wrist. With no destination in mind, she drove with the desire to just simply go. It wasn't until she parked that she realized where she'd gone. Rain drizzled against the windshield as she stared through its glistening drops up at the hospital. Maybe she should have called first and inquired about Edwards's condition.

But what if she ran into Nathan? What would she say—"Hi. My name is C.J. Cartel and I may have killed your father"? She shook the thought from her head. *I'll just go in and ask one of the nurses how Travis is doing, then I'll leave,* she reasoned.

Looking around, she realized that she'd left her umbrella at the office. She climbed out of the car and decided to make a run for it. The thin sheets of rain quickly became fat pelts, pounding her mercilessly. By the time she'd reached the portico leading to the entrance, there wasn't a dry spot on her body.

Shivering beneath the overworked air conditioner, she searched for the nearest restroom. One look in the mirror and she concluded that the term *drowned rat* was too good for her. With more than her fair share of paper towels, she dried off as best she could. The result was horrifying. Her hair was a frizzled mess and her clothes qualified her to enter a wet T-shirt contest. It was the perfect ending for the perfect day.

With some work, she managed to pull her hair back in its usual bun, but her clothes were hopeless. When she walked out of the bathroom, she received more than her fair share of curious stares. *Just find the ICU, ask your question, and get the hell out of here,* she told herself. But she'd entered the hospital from a different entrance and had quickly gotten lost. The waft of fresh coffee caught her attention and drew her toward the cafeteria, where the temptation of something warm convinced her to make a quick detour.

Nathan sat in the corner of the cafeteria, staring down into a cup of black liquid, wishing that he were somewhere else. He'd been at the hospital for more than seventeen hours and wondered how much longer he intended to stay.

He sighed and glanced out the corner of his eye. *What on earth?* A flare of recognition lit his eyes as he stared at the woman from this morning, but he could hardly believe what he was seeing.

He stood, unsure of what he intended to say, and headed toward her. When he stopped behind her, it was then that he realized that he didn't know the woman's name.

Carissa dug in her purse, alarmed when she couldn't find any cash. "I don't believe this."

The bored cashier expelled an irritated sigh and rolled her heavily made-up eyes heavenward.

"Just a sec. I know I at least have some change somewhere in here."

As if accustomed to this incident happening, Bettye, as the name tag read, started to void the ticket.

"I've got it."

Carissa jumped, then turned toward the rich baritone. She sucked in a deep breath the moment her brain registered the man's identity.

Nathan handed Bettye a dollar and instructed her to "keep the change." He then turned his smile toward Carissa.

She jerked her body around, gathered her things, and shoved it all back into her purse. Embarrassment burned at the roots of her hair and she grabbed the dispoable cup with too much force. The scalding liquid sloshed over the rim and splashed against her hand.

"Damn it!" Carissa released the cup. Both she and Bettye jumped back as it dropped against the counter and coffee sprayed everywhere.

Nathan caught the brunt of her weight. Luckily,

his footing was sure enough to prevent them from falling backward.

Bettye's nostrils flared with anger while her hands balled into fists at her sides.

"I'm sorry," Carissa said, rushing forward. The apology sounded strange to her own ears.

"Sweetheart, why don't you go and sit down while I help Bettye clean this up?" Nathan intervened.

Carissa's spine stiffened. "Sweetheart?" The word trickled like acid from her lips.

His left brow arched and she read in his expression that it was a silent command. And to her own utter amazement, she conceded and obeyed the order.

Five minutes later, with her temper still ablaze, the insufferable man joined her at a table in the far corner of the cafeteria with two steaming cups of coffee.

"I see you made it to a table without any further incidents." He placed a cup in front of her.

Whether he meant the statement as a joke or not, she couldn't tell. "I suppose you expect me to thank you for humiliating me like that?"

"Who, me?" This time when his brows arched, she saw nothing but amusement covering his features, and her anger boiled.

"Yes, you. You ordered me around in front of that woman like I was a brainless idiot."

He frowned at her. "I did no such thing."

"You damn well did and I don't appreciate it."

He sat still and stared at her before he spoke again. "Lady, I don't know whether you're dealing with a full deck or not. But all *I* seem to remember is me keeping you from making a bigger fool of yourself."

Her mouth opened and closed in a series of gasps, but she never quite found her voice.

"If you're trying to win this argument, I think you actually have to say something." He leaned back. "Maybe something rude. It does seem to be your forte."

"Kiss off."

"That's my girl. Do you feel any better?"

"First of all, I'm *not* your girl."

"And here I thought God had stopped performing miracles."

Red, brilliant in all its glory, flashed before her eyes. She counted to ten. When that didn't work, she tried ten more.

He laughed then. "Do you always go through such extremes to avoid thanking someone?"

Jaws clenched, Carissa glared at him.

"Ah, you're going to give me the silent treatment. That's kind of childish, don't you think?"

"Mr. Edwards," she began in a controlled tone. "From the moment I laid eyes on you, you've done nothing but insult and humiliate me."

"That must be your favorite word—*humiliate*."

"Can I please finish?"

"By all means." He crossed his arms.

His corded muscles flexed and relaxed, causing her train of thought to jump tracks. "Oh, forget it. I don't know why I'm wasting my time." She stood.

Nathan's hand shot out and grabbed her wrist. "Wait." Frustration marred his features. "I'm sorry."

She waited, halfway hoping he'd grovel for forgiveness. Instead, he held her gaze, and before she knew it, she was swept into a vortex of electrical currents from more than just his eyes. It streamed from his touch and the air that surrounded them.

Pulling her hand back, she drew in small puffs of air through her lips, but was unwilling to break eye contact. What she was feeling frightened and confused her.

"Won't you please stay?" he asked.

She nodded before her brain had a chance to register the question.

"Maybe we should start over and introduce ourselves. My name is Nathan Edwards."

"Carissa Car—" She caught herself as this morning's dream flashed before her eyes—the accusation, the pain and *his* hatred. If he knew she'd caused his father's attack, that dream would become a reality.

"I didn't quite catch your last name."

Her awkward smile wobbled at the corners. "Uh, Carnes. Carissa Carnes."

His massive hands swallowed hers. "It's nice to officially meet you, Ms. Carnes."

Perfect rows of white, even teeth flashed her. Their sudden appearance transformed his masculine features into something breathtaking. She never thought a man could be described as beautiful before, but that is how she thought of Nathan Edwards now. Simply beautiful.

He held her hand longer than necessary before finally releasing it.

Remembering her wild appearance, another rush of embarrassment burned her face. "I know I look a fright. I got caught out in the rain."

"You look fine."

"You're a good liar."

"Now that's the first time I've been accused of that. Most of my friends call me Honest Abe." His rich laugh accelerated her heartbeat and she knew then that she was in trouble. There were too many things she found fascinating about him, too many things that made her body respond. She reached for her cup. "Thank you again for the coffee."

"Again?"

This time, she laughed, and it felt good. "All right, you win. Thank you."

"I don't know you, but I have a feeling that was probably the hardest thing you've ever done."

You have no idea. Smiling, she sipped her coffee.

"So—" his voice turned serious "—just how *do* you know my father?"

Carissa choked.

Chapter 8

Nathan leaned forward to help Carissa, but stopped when she held up a hand. "I'm okay." She cleared her throat, then wiped her eyes. All the while, her mind raced for a response—or rather a lie.

"Are you sure?"

Avoiding his dark gaze, she nodded. "It probably just went down the wrong pipe."

He watched her, then shook his head in bewilderment. "I'm not quite sure what to make of you."

"What do you mean?" She welcomed the change of topic.

"I don't know." He shrugged. "One minute you come across as a strong, independent woman. You don't need anything or anyone. I bet you'll challenge anyone to prove otherwise. Then, you flip mode."

"Flip mode?"

Nathan smiled. "Yeah, flip the switch, change gears and appear childlike—insecure, vulnerable. I'm not sure what to make of it."

Her eyes narrowed. "How old are you?"

His head drew back with a bark of laughter. "Since when is that a politically correct thing to ask?"

"You have it all wrong. I'm well within my legal bounds. A man can never ask a woman that question, but it's okay for us to ask."

"Is that right?"

"Yeah, that's right." She smiled as if it made perfect sense. "I mean, I'm just curious. You have the manners of a two-year-old and you talk like a Generation X wannabe."

"You sound interested."

"And apparently you're a hopeless daydreamer."

He laughed and couldn't remember the last time he'd enjoyed someone's company this much. "You know you have a wonderful gift," he said, meeting her gaze.

"What's that?"

"Helping me forget my worries."

"Now that's the first time *I've* heard that one." She lowered her gaze and struggled to swallow the lump of guilt lodged in her throat. Her confession edged to the tip of her tongue, when he reached across the table and covered her hand with his.

"Thank you." Thick, raw emotion layered the two simple words. "I'm glad you're here. It's apparent that you really care for my father or you wouldn't be here at this hour."

Tell him the truth. But she couldn't. The pain in his eyes and its intensity prevented her. She placed her free hand atop his. "I had to come."

The ensuing silence hugged the couple and consoled their troubled thoughts. It was wrong to lead him on this way. Since when was she scared of the truth? Why was hurting this man such an abominable thought?

"Do you know what I keep thinking about?"

His question was so low she barely heard it. She shook her head.

"My mother." He squeezed her hand. "I was devastated when I lost her."

Orphaned by death herself, she drew in a shaky breath and winced at the sudden constriction of her heart muscles. "When?" she whispered.

"Three years ago—on a Sunday."

Her vision blurred.

"How about you?"

"Sundays." She wiped away a tear before it escaped her eyes. "How did you know?"

"I sensed it."

"Your father is going to pull through," she confirmed with a nod. "I just know it." Like hell she did, but the thought of the alternative left a rancid taste in her mouth.

A bond had formed between them. She couldn't pinpoint when or how it happened, but she felt it, and she was surprised by its strength.

She watched him struggle with his next question. "Has he ever told you about me?"

Treading on dangerous ground, and still unwilling to risk causing more pain, she continued to weave her deceptive web. "Only that he loves you."

His hand went cold and Nathan pulled away.

She'd crossed the line and a heartfelt apology tumbled from her lips.

"It's all right. It's not your fault." He dismissed her ramblings with a firm head shake. "I'm just fighting with one hell of a guilty conscience. I'm sure you know I've refused to have any contact with my father. Mainly because I thought it was too late. Like a he-made-his-bed-and-now-he-has-to-lie-in-it sort of philosophy."

Their eyes met again and Carissa was drawn in by more than his words. *Oh, God. What am I doing?*

"I guess I just wanted to hurt him." Anger flashed in his expressive eyes.

Carissa understood all too well that burning desire to punish the very ones you love. "You wasted your time," she said. "In the end, you only succeed in hurting yourself."

Nodding as if he'd already discovered that fact, he added, "I still don't know what the answer is. What was I supposed to do—forget what happened and let him waltz back into my life with open arms? I don't understand why this is my burden to bear."

"I don't have all the answers." She attempted to pacify him. "Trust me, I'm the last person you should take advice from. I've spent nearly two decades trying to appease my guilt, wishing like hell I could just turn back the clock and erase the pain I caused, take back those angry words I didn't mean." Her voice trailed to a whisper.

It felt good to unburden her past, to finally tell someone of the hell she'd been through. "I have to tell you, if anything, I envy you. You still have a chance to set things right."

"You make it all sound so easy."

"Maybe it is."

He nodded at that, then was unable to say anything else.

"It's amazing how many times the same questions can cross your mind, isn't it?" she finally asked.

"Yeah."

She felt, rather than witnessed, him surrender to his inner turmoil, and she was helpless to do anything for him. Glancing at the clock, she was shocked by the time. "I should go. It's late—or rather it's early." Her announcement pulled him out of his troubled reverie.

"Do you really have to go?"

It was those eyes again that tugged at her. "Well, I guess I could stay a little longer." She wouldn't leave him now if Congress decreed it as law.

"Thank you," he said in a voice that had her fantasizing of its sound drifting lazily across her ears at the peak of passion. Again, she wondered what in the *hell* was wrong with her.

Nathan studied Carissa and thought his father was a very lucky man. Who was this beautiful woman with the woman-child eyes? Why did the thought of her leaving trouble him? They were kindred spirits. That much was evident—there were too many commonalities between them. He remembered what she'd looked like with her hair down and wondered why she kept it pulled back in that ridiculous bun. What he wouldn't give to have her in his studio for one day. His camera would love her.

He watched her take a sip of her cold coffee and enjoyed the way her nose wrinkled at the discovery. "Would you like another cup?"

"No, that won't be necessary. I've drunk too much of this stuff anyway."

"That makes two of us. The difference is I have no intentions of quitting."

She laughed, and he loved its melodious sound. "Well, the way I see it," he continued, "it's better than the other vices. I don't drink, smoke or do drugs. I'm not even a compulsive womanizer."

"Why? Do you like men?"

He laughed. "Okay, that's one for you."

"Is that a no?"

"It's a hell no."

"Doesn't hurt to ask."

"Why? Are you still interested?"

"Only if you're still daydreaming."

They talked for what seemed like eternity. Nathan appreciated her patience, and he believed she understood what he was going through. Vaguely, he was aware that she remained aloof about details of her own life. However, it was to be expected. They hardly knew each other. Then why was it that *he* couldn't shut up?

Had years of suppressed emotions finally taken their toll? He wasn't sure and didn't really care to question why he was comfortable around her. He just knew that it felt good to finally talk to someone.

When the clock ticked closer toward six in the morning, he watched with amusement as she struggled to ward off her drowsiness. The writing was on the wall. It was time for their wonderful morning to end.

He escorted her to her car, impressed by the make and model. It occurred to him then that he didn't have the slightest idea what she did for a living.

Carissa unlocked the door.

"Are you sure you're going to be able to drive home?"

She stifled a yawn behind her hand, then nodded. "What about you? Are you going to get some sleep, too?"

An image of him lying next to her surfaced in his mind. He smiled. "I do need to go home and clean up."

"There's that and you can't live off coffee alone."

"You're right. We should have lunch."

"Not possible."

He caught the regret in her voice. "Dinner, then?"

She shook her head.

"I would love to talk to you again," he added before she voiced an answer.

When she hesitated, he gave his best puppy dog expression. "I'm sorry, but I can't."

The rejection bruised his ego, but he shrugged it off. "I understand. I'm probably coming on too strong. Maybe I'll see you around."

Nathan shut her door as she started the car. Even now he didn't want her to go, but he smiled—at least he hoped it was a smile, and felt something akin to hope when she returned the gesture.

She rolled down the window. "Goodbye," she said, then pulled off.

He watched the utility vehicle until it faded from view, drew in a cleansing breath and wondered aloud, "What in the hell has gotten into me?"

Chapter 9

Liz glanced into the rearview mirror at Darius, who sat secured in the backseat. "Baby, why don't you talk with the other children?"

He shrugged, then lowered his head and pretended to be fascinated with his hands.

"Sweetheart, Mommy's not angry. I'm just trying to understand. You always talk at home. Do you not like the other children?"

He shrugged.

"Is it your teachers?"

Another shrug.

She hated it when he did that, hated how it made her feel. It was too much. She was already dealing with a full plate: a stressful job, Nana's illness, her ex-husband's missing child-support checks, now Darius's what? What was this—a game, a cry for help or just an attention grabber?

"Darius, please tell me what's wrong."

He remained silent for so long, she thought he wouldn't answer, but when he did, it was in a voice that was smaller than normal.

"I don't think they like me."

His conclusion broke her heart. "Oh, baby. I'm sure that's not true."

"It feels like it is."

What could she do—change day care, again? It was already the fifth one this year. "Tell me why you believe that."

He sniffed then, and she looked over at him and discovered him crying. And by the time she pulled into the day care, she was crying, too.

Nathan's battle with exhaustion waned to a close. He needed sleep and soon. "You can't live off coffee alone," he quoted Carissa with a smile. Again, he marveled over the strange combination of fire and ice in her personality and concluded that it must be what drew him toward her. Who knew? Maybe getting to know her would help him better understand his father.

And he needed to understand.

Entering his father's unit, he approached the bed attuned to the steady beep from the heart monitor.

Dr. Peterson had informed him that there were no changes in his father's condition, which wasn't good or bad news. It was just what it was—nothing. Nathan placed his hand against his father's and hated its coldness.

"I have to be honest with you," the doctor's voice echoed in his head. "There's a chance that he may never recover."

Nathan shook away yesterday's conversation, refusing to acknowledge the possibility.

A nurse breezed into the unit.

Nathan blinked his eyes dry and erased any evidence of his emotional torment.

"How are we today?" she asked in an exaggerated Southern drawl. When she looked up to meet his gaze, her expression sobered. "I'll only take a moment," she assured him, then changed the IV.

Something flickered in Nathan's peripheral vision. He stared back at his father and waited for it to happen again.

Travis's eyelids twitched.

"He moved," he said, excited.

"Involuntary movements are common for coma patients," the nurse assured him with a sympathetic smile.

Nathan's excitement lulled and his heartbeat returned to normal. But he couldn't help but feel that something was happening behind his father's lids...

Duc Pho, South Vietnam, 1968

Travis thought he was dying.

The round he took just below his rib cage shot pain throughout his body, making him oblivious to the continuing gunfire that surrounded him.

The past few hours passed before his eyes. He was the battalion S3, the officer in charge of planning operations. Then suddenly rockets and mortars shelled the base. Now, after a cruel twist of fate, he was the action battalion commander.

"Sir, are you all right?" a soldier in his platoon shouted close by. He recognized Tony's voice instantly.

A native of the Bronx, Tony's street sense gave him an edge in the bush. He boasted he loved to fight. It may have been true—or it may have been his way of coping.

Travis managed to nod, while gasping for air—for life. He tasted his salty tears, then clenched his jaw when the soldier lifted him and trotted across the field. Each bounce inched him closer to the void spreading in his mind.

"Incoming!"

The scream came from the other side of the perimeter when the unmistakable crack of AK-47 rifles filled the morning air. His earlier speculation was confirmed. This wasn't harassment fire, but an organized attack. NVA regulars. He expected Charlie and Alpha Company would make heavy contact in the bush, but a direct attack on this position had caught them off guard.

Suddenly, he was airborne, drifting across the field as if defying gravity. Pain ricocheted throughout his body upon first impact and a black haze swallowed him, but he broke through the surface, once again struggling for breath.

Where was Tony? He turned his head and found the young man sprawled across the dirt. His lifeless gaze stared straight at him while blood trickled from the hole in the center of his forehead.

Travis looked away, trying to block the image from his mind. Visions of his wife and his two-year-old son stared back at him through the darkness. He was never going to hold her in his arms again, never see his son grow old.

A sob tore from his throat. His body trembled in anguish. "Please, God," he prayed, then allowed his tears to flow. The battle drifted off into the distance. His heartbeat, loud and hard, was the only sound he heard. And it soothed him, blossoming a peace he'd never known.

Desire, strong and true, filled him, and he opened his eyes. The strength he'd thought had long abandoned him had returned. That, along with sheer determination, forced him to use his arms and pull his body in a slow crawl across the field, where he'd hoped to find safety.

His vision faded in and out of focus, but he kept going—and believed he would see his family again.

Chapter 10

"What a night." Carissa sighed as she closed her front door and slumped behind it. What in the hell was she doing? She'd dug a nice little grave for herself, that was what. Now how was she going to get out of this one?

The door pushed open from behind her and she jumped away in surprise. When her aunt eased her head inside, Carissa eyed her with astonishment.

"Please tell me you're not just getting home."

Helena smiled and closed the door behind her, but before she responded, she cast a futile glance over her niece's attire. "I see I'm not the only one just getting in."

"I spent the night at the hospital. Where were you?"

Helena smiled wickedly. "I'll tell you when you're older."

Carissa shook her head. "You'll never change."

"Change? God forbid. I'm in the prime of my life. And unlike you, I'm still determined to find my Prince Charming." She sashayed past Carissa, whistling.

"What are you talking about? You've been married six times."

"Yeah. Come on, lucky number seven," Helena sang, entering the kitchen and heading straight for the coffeemaker. "Good. I see the maid service cleaned up the mess." She opened a cabinet.

"Wait," Carissa commanded.

Her aunt pivoted with her brows raised in curiosity. "Is there a problem?"

"Do you know how to work a coffeemaker?"

"Give me a break." Helena laughed. "How difficult can it be?"

"I'll do it," Carissa insisted, before taking over the task.

"Whatever floats your boat." Helena shrugged off the insult, then sat on the stool by the credenza. "Now tell me what on earth kept you at the hospital all night?"

Carissa's back stiffened. "There's nothing to tell. I went to see about Mr. Edwards's condition."

"And it took all night?" Helena's disbelief echoed in her voice. "Are you sure Junior doesn't have anything to do with your extended interest in this situation?"

"His name is Nathan. And don't be silly." Carissa shook her head, but didn't dare turn around to meet her aunt's gaze.

Helena laughed. "You have to do better than that if you're going to try to lie to me, sweetie. Don't forget my maiden name is Cartel, too."

"Be that as it may," Carissa said as she hit the brew button, then turned to face her aunt, "you're still barking up the wrong tree. What I'm dealing with is just a tremendous amount of guilt. It's nothing more than that." She sat next to Helena with a tight smile.

"Guilt, huh? Now what do you have to feel guilty about? From what I've heard, you've been known to eat businessmen like Edwards for breakfast. Why the sudden concern?"

"Because I've never been responsible for any of them lying in a coma."

"You're overreacting and you know it."

"No, I don't. Excuse me for growing a heart."

Helena held her hands up in surrender. "Touché. I apologize. I'm just trying to understand what's going on in that busy little head of yours. And believe me, I'm not the least bit disappointed that you've decided to grow a heart. Frankly, I think it's about time."

"Please, I'm not in the mood for a speech." Carissa groaned as she exhaled. "I don't mean to be rude."

"Well, you're doing a damn good job of it."

Carissa's frustration mounted. "I'm thirty-two

years old, Auntie. When do you think you'll stop advising me how to run my life?"

"Excuse me for trying to help."

Silence trailed Helena's curt tone and Carissa buried her head in her hands. "I'm sorry. I don't know what's wrong with me."

Helena shrugged. "Well, I do. And it sounds to me that you do, too. The question now is when are you going to come clean with this Nathan character."

Exhausted, Nathan arrived at his apartment in the center of downtown Atlanta with the idea of grabbing a quick shower and a nap. But no sooner had he eased inside the door than the sound of running water stole his attention.

Someone's taking a shower. His brows furrowed as he looked around. He was in the right apartment, he concluded. He moved farther into the room. Whoever was in the bathroom had apparently made themselves at home. The scent of freshly brewed coffee drifted throughout the apartment.

He peeked into the kitchen to see dishes piled in the sink and magazines scattered across the counters.

The shower cut off and Nathan's attention turned toward the bedroom. A familiar feminine voice began singing and he knew instantly who his uninvited guest was.

Nathan stood with his arms crossed and waited for the bedroom door to swing open. When it did, the singing stopped.

"Hello, India." His gaze quickly took in her wet, ink-black hair and flawless honey-brown complexion. She was still as beautiful as he remembered.

"Nathan. What are you doing here?" She tightened her hold on the towel wrapped around her body.

"Don't you think that you should be answering that question?" He watched as she swallowed hard and shifted her weight nervously.

She stood staring at him as if dumbstruck.

He waved his hand in front of her face. "Hello?"

"I'm sorry. I know I should have checked with you about staying in here, but I knew you rarely came to Atlanta this time of year, and I guess I was afraid that you would say no."

"You were right." He walked away. "How fast can you move out?" he asked with his back to her. The memory of her betrayal resurfaced in his mind.

"So it's just like that? You're just going to throw me out?"

"India, it's over. It's been over." He faced her, but then looked away when her eyes glossed over. "Don't do this," he warned.

"Why can't you forgive me? I made a mistake. And for that you're willing to throw away a five-year relationship?"

"Will you please put some damn clothes on," he yelled. "I can't think with you dressed like that."

She stepped forward. "Maybe I don't want you to think. It seems like every time you go off thinking I'm the one that ends up getting hurt."

"Funny. I seem to remember your lies hurting me."

She took another step forward.

"It's not going to happen." His glare stopped her in her tracks.

A long painful silence enveloped them before Nathan spoke again. "This is the last thing I need. I can't deal with you right now."

She recoiled as if he'd slapped her.

"You're a hard man, Nathan Edwards. And you can be quite unforgiving, too."

"Is that what you think—that I haven't forgiven you?" This time he moved to close the gap. "I forgave you a long time ago. The problem is I can't forget."

India looked deep into his eyes and lifted her hand to caress his face. On her finger, the engagement ring he allowed her to keep sparkled. "I know you still love me," she whispered.

He nodded. "I won't lie to you. I do still care for you. But I can't build a life without trust. And the woman that I marry I need to be able to trust completely."

Chapter 11

Carissa bolted upright at the phone's sudden shrill. Sunlight stabbed her eyes and she immediately slammed them shut again. *What time is it?*

When the phone rang again, she snatched the receiver off the cradle. "Hello." Her voice croaked over the line. She coughed to clear it.

"Ms. Cartel?" Liz questioned.

"Yes. What is it?" She looked around to find the clock. It was well past one in the afternoon. She'd slept in two days in a row. That had to be a record. "Is there something wrong?" she asked.

"Uh, no. It's nothing like that. I figured you'd want to know that Nathan Edwards, Travis Edwards's son, has arrived in town."

"Yeah, I know. I ran into him a couple of times yesterday." Carissa swung her legs out of bed, but made no attempt to stand. "Luckily for me, he has no idea who I am and I intend to keep it that way."

"Oh."

Carissa frowned. "What does 'oh' mean?"

"Well, I think you should know that Mr. Edwards had called here at the office asking questions."

"When? What did he want to know?" she asked, jumping to her feet and pacing in front of the nightstand.

"He called yesterday. He's coming by the office today."

"I left a message on your desk, but when I went in your office a few minutes ago I saw you hadn't gone through all of them yet."

Liz was right. She hadn't read all of her messages. "Damn." Carissa's mind raced. "No doubt he'll want to know what happened the other day."

"He has the right to know."

"Of course he does. I'm not saying he doesn't. I just don't think that it's a good idea that he hears it from me. Especially since he thinks I'm someone else." She thought for a moment. "So much for getting through this incognito."

"Actually, he called here wanting to talk to me."

"What?"

"Well, I am the one who'd called. I don't mind talking to him as long as you're okay with it. Besides, he should be here soon and you'll never be able to get here on time."

Carissa hesitated. It was the coward's way out. "Are you sure?"

"Yeah. I'll handle it. Like I said. I called, I should handle it."

"Thanks, Liz. I owe you big-time."

When the women hung up, Carissa stood and stared at the phone. A sliver of guilt eased its way into her conscience. She was behaving as if she *had* murdered someone.

She remembered her long talk with Nathan. They had a lot in common to be so different. Even though Nathan and Travis weren't exactly close, she still didn't want yesterday's nightmare to come true. Besides, maybe she could stop Nathan from making the same mistakes she'd made.

She sat back on the edge of the bed. "Who am I, Dr. Laura?" she said, shaking her head. "I'm definitely losing it."

A soft knock sounded at the door. "Carissa, sweetheart. Are you up?" Helena asked.

"Does that woman ever sleep?" she mumbled to herself.

The door swung open.

"I heard that," Helena said, sweeping into the room like a breath of fresh air. Her tightly coiled hair and flawless skin helped her appear twenty years younger. "Unlike you, I don't intend to sleep this beautiful day away. I've already made plans on what we're going to do for the rest of the day."

"Plans? Oh, I don't know, Auntie. I have a million

things to do." She moved from the bed and headed toward the bathroom.

"Come on, Risa. I'm sure those things can wait. Let's go shopping, take in a matinee, then paint the town red when the sun goes down."

Carissa turned and laughed. "Where on earth do you get your energy from at your age?"

"I have the same amount of energy as you do. I just direct it toward enjoying life instead of leaping tall buildings in a single bound."

"Hey, I enjoy my life, too. I mean, sure I have my ups and downs, but for the most part, I know how to have a good time."

"Prove it."

Carissa fell speechless at the challenge. "All right, all right. You win. Maybe a day out on the town is just what I need."

Helena's smile widened. "Great. Hurry up and get dressed. I read in the paper than Nieman-Marcus is having some type of sale today and I want to try that new Justin's restaurant out in Buckhead tonight."

"Great." Carissa exaggerated her enthusiasm and watched her aunt saunter out of the room. *Where in the hell did she learn to walk like that? And where can I take lessons?*

"I can't believe she just made herself at home," Nathan said, handing his stepfather, Smokey, a beer. "She has a lot of nerve."

"Believe it or not there are a lot of worse things a

man can come home to than a naked woman in his shower. Hell, I wish I had your kind of luck."

"You're missing the point, Pop." Nathan plopped down beside him on the couch, wearing only a pair of black jeans.

"Well, I'll be damned." Smokey pointed to Nathan's arm. "When did you get a tattoo?" He referred to the malicious-looking panther posed over Nathan's large biceps.

"That happened after a dare and one too many bottles of Jack Daniels."

"You still can't walk away from a dare?"

"I've walked away from a few." The men laughed, then continued their private drink.

"So what exactly happened between you and India, anyway? Or are you planning on keeping it a big secret?"

Nathan was quiet for a moment. His thoughts were instantly tangled in the past. "There was always some type of problem happening. At first they were small. She'd tell me she was doing one thing, then I'd find out that she'd done another. I don't know, there just seemed to be a lot of unnecessary lies." He shrugged. "Then the lies got bigger and the next thing I know, she's sleeping around. And I do mean around."

"I'm sorry, son." Smokey slapped his back, then shook his head. "Damn. I didn't figure her to be the type."

"Pop, if I've learned anything about women, it's you can never know their type until it's too late."

"It sounds like this one left you a little bitter."

For some odd reason, Nathan thought of Carissa. "I don't know if *bitter* is the word I'm looking for. More like *cautious.*"

"Now if *I've* learned anything over the years, it would be that a man can never be too cautious."

"Here, here."

The men's bottles clinked together in a quick toast.

"What time are you going back to the hospital?"

The question sounded awkward to Nathan's ears, but he understood his stepfather's position and knew his concern was only for his benefit. Nathan looked at his watch. "I planned to head back out there in about an hour."

"Planning on another all-nighter?"

"I don't think I can handle too many more of those. But I'll stay as long as the body allows."

The men nursed their beers in silence, while each wondered what the other was thinking.

"I know what you're trying to do is probably the right thing," Smokey began. "But I have to say I'm kind of surprised."

"No more than I am." Nathan cleared his throat. "I just know that I'll regret it for the rest of my life if I walk away from him now."

"It's not like he's been there for you or your mother," he sneered.

"I know, but two wrongs don't make a right." Nathan stood and moved away. "I was talking with his fiancée at the hospital last night and—"

"His fiancée?"

"Yeah, if you can believe it." Nathan shared a half laugh. "She has to be my age, too. I have to hand it to him—she's beautiful. Maybe a little uptight, but a definite looker."

Smokey lifted a curious brow. "She seems to have made quite an impression on you."

Nathan shrugged. "She has. I'm actually happy that she was there last night. She helped me talk through a lot of things—a lot of feelings I didn't know I had."

The men fell silent again.

Smokey stood. "I guess I better get going."

"You don't have to go now." Nathan feared that he'd hurt his feelings somehow, but was at a loss as to how to mend them.

"Don't worry about me. I have a ton of things to do at the office."

"How is that new job going anyway? What's the name of the company?"

Smokey laughed, then landed another hard slap across Nathan's back. "What's this? A sudden interest in corporate America?"

"Heaven forbid. I'm just trying to keep you from walking out the door mad."

They stood smiling at each other.

"All right. I admit I'm a little concerned about what's going on between you and Travis. I just don't want to see you get hurt."

"I'm a grown man now, Pop."

"You can still get hurt."

"I guess that's a chance I'm going to have to take. Don't worry," Nathan said, returning the affectionate slap on the back. "I'm not trying to replace you. You'll always be my father. You're the one that has always been here for me."

A genuine smile lit Smokey's eyes. "Thanks, son. I needed to hear that."

"Good. Then what do you say we get together for dinner tonight? And don't tell me about your workaholic schedule. Surely you can squeeze in time to have dinner with your son."

"All right. You're on. How about we meet at Justin's. It's not too far from the office. Say around eight?"

"Eight it is."

Chapter 12

Liz spent the day thankful Carissa hadn't come into the office. Since she hadn't had time to find a new day care, she had no choice but to bring Darius to work with her. As usual, he remained quiet and stayed out of the way for most of the day. Whenever a coworker attempted to speak to him, he'd retreat behind his mother's chair and refuse to speak.

Liz was at a loss to explain his behavior.

"Well, he seems to be a sweet boy," Adelle replied, shaking her head. "He'll grow out of it. I know my son was shy at his age. By the time he reached five, he'd turned into a hellion."

"Darius *is* five." Liz exhaled.

"Oh."

"But maybe you're right. He can still grow out of it," Liz said, looking up to her coworker and friend. "There are days I have my doubt. I wonder if it's because there isn't a father figure in his life."

"Now, honey, don't go blaming yourself. Everything will work out. Take my word on it." Adelle patted her hand and strode off.

Darius eased from behind her chair and returned to the coloring book spread out at the end of her desk. Sadly, she watched him out of the corner of her eye. Maybe she should check into taking him to a child psychologist.

Expelling a frustrated sigh, she wondered where on earth she'd find money for that in her budget. Lord, she was tired. Between her job, her grandmother and Darius, the candle she burned at both ends had finally met in the center.

"Well, baby, it's almost five o'clock. Mommy has to run these reports over to Hunter's secretary, then we can go home. Can you sit here and be a good boy until I get back?"

Darius looked up and nodded. "Are we still going to McDonald's on the way home?"

"Yes, sir. A promise is a promise," she said, standing. "I'll be right back."

Quietly, Darius began putting his crayons back into the box. But no sooner had his mother turned the corner than a heavy baritone voice caused him to jump out of his skin.

"Hello there, little fella," Nathan greeted him,

smiling down at the boy. "Can you tell me where I can find a Ms. Townsend?"

The boy just stared up at him.

"I was told her office was up here." Nathan frowned. "Do you happen to know who I'm talking about?"

Still there was no response.

"Okay." Nathan rubbed the side of his head to ensure he hadn't grown an extra head. "I bet your mommy taught you not to talk to strangers, didn't she?"

To his amazement, the boy nodded.

"Well, that's a good rule. I'm sure your mommy is very proud of you for being obedient." He gave the boy a genuine smile. "Now it seems I still have a bit of a problem. I'm lost and I really don't want you to get in trouble with your mother." Nathan stroked his chin as if in deep thought, and then he noticed the coloring book.

"I know." He snapped his fingers. "How about you draw me a map to Ms. Townsend's desk. You think you can do that?"

Darius smiled, then shook his head.

Nathan playfully eyed him suspiciously. "I'm beginning to think that you don't even know Ms. Townsend."

"Yes, I do," Darius blurted out, then slapped his small hand across his mouth.

Nathan mimicked him. "Uh-oh. You spoke."

Darius giggled behind his hand.

"I guess that means that you have to go ahead and tell me where this Ms. Townsend is."

The boy's eyes seemed to twinkle during the brief silence.

"She's my mommy."

"Well, how about that." Nathan crossed his arms while maintaining his smile. "I would have never thought that Ms. Townsend had raised such an impressive-looking young man. You must be what—eight years old?"

"Five."

"Is that right?"

"I don't believe what I'm hearing."

Nathan looked up to see an attractive woman approaching them, smiling.

"My son never speaks to strangers."

"I'm sorry. I didn't mean to get the little man in any trouble."

Darius grabbed his mother's hand. "He said he was looking for you, Mommy."

"Is that right?"

Nathan watched the exchange, puzzled by the woman's sudden tears. "Ma'am, I didn't mean to upset you."

"No, no. You haven't upset me." She sat behind the desk and reached for a tissue.

"That remains to be seen," he mumbled under his breath.

"Oh, Mommy is so proud of you." She pulled her son into a fierce hug and rocked with him.

Nathan looked around, half expecting a camera crew to announce that he was the subject of some practical joke.

"I'm sorry. Where are my manners?" she asked, releasing her son and offering him her hand. "I'm Elizabeth Townsend, C. J. Cartel's administrative assistant. You must be Nathan Edwards."

He accepted her hand. "How did you guess?"

"You bear a striking resemblance to your father."

Their hands lowered as Nathan nodded.

"I want to thank you for agreeing to speak with me. I know it may seem a bit odd, but I just want to know what happened." He noticed her smile falter, but it quickly returned.

"Won't you have a seat?" She gestured to a chair to the right of her desk.

She was stalling, he knew, but he managed to return her smile and accept her offer. "Thank you."

"Well, there isn't much to tell," she began. "Cartel Enterprises has recently acquired your father's company, Edwards Electronics. However, Mr. Edwards wasn't too happy about the acquisition."

"So it was like a hostile takeover?"

"I guess you can say that."

He could tell the conversation made her uneasy. "Then what happened?"

"Mr. Edwards came here pretty irate the other day and stormed past me to see Cartel. For a couple of minutes I could hear him yelling from my desk."

"So they were in a heated argument?"

Liz shook her head. "Cartel is not one to yell. And like I said, your father's voice was the only one I heard out here."

Nathan pictured this Cartel to be one tough businessman. In the back of his mind, he wondered where he'd heard the name C. J. Cartel before.

"Anyway," Liz continued, "the next thing I know, the office was quiet. A minute later, my boss buzzed me over the intercom to call 911."

"I see," he said, crossing his arms. He stared at her to evaluate whether there was something she wasn't telling him.

"I wish there were more I could tell you." Her sympathetic gaze returned his stare.

"Where is your boss now?"

Liz blinked. "Cartel's not in today."

"When will he be in?"

She hesitated, and he wondered what she was hiding. "I'm not sure."

"Is he out of town?"

"I'm not sure."

"You're not sure?" He thought of Gina and couldn't imagine her not knowing where he was at all times. "I tell you what. Why don't I leave my name and number and you can relay to your boss that I would like to schedule a meeting with him." He smiled. "If that isn't too much to ask."

Liz nodded and took down the information. "I'll make sure that he gets this."

"Thank you." His gaze shifted to her son. "I'll see you around, little man."

Darius smiled. "Bye."

Liz's mouth fell open.

Carissa was exhausted. She hated shopping—always had. And after her aunt had dragged her to more than a dozen stores, her feelings were reinforced. Especially since, in the end, they only purchased a bottle of her aunt's favorite perfume.

By the time they arrived at Justin's, she was famished.

"I'm having a wonderful time," Helena said, picking up a menu. "After we eat here, I'd like to go over to Club Mirage. I hear the Black Chippendales are performing tonight."

"You want to go to a club—to see strippers?" Carissa asked, astonished.

Helena chuckled. "Don't tell me that the party train has rolled to a stop. I thought we were going to paint the town red tonight."

Carissa held up her hand. "Okay, okay. A promise is a promise."

"Good." Pleased, Helena smiled. "Trust me. We're going to have a great time."

"I just bet we are."

"Sweetheart, why don't you ever wear your hair down? You have beautiful hair."

"Thanks. But I like it up."

"You're too uptight. I'm going to make it my personal goal to loosen you up by the time I leave."

"Is that right?"

"I see I have my work cut out for me. But I've never been able to walk away from a challenge."

Carissa laughed. "At least we have one thing in common."

A waiter appeared. "Can I get you ladies something to drink?"

While Helena placed their drink orders, a familiar face caught Carissa's attention out of the corner of her eye. When she leaned over to get a better view around her aunt, the image disappeared.

"What is it?" Helena turned to follow her gaze.

"I guess nothing." Carissa shrugged. "I just thought I saw my VP. That's all."

"I know what you need." Helena clapped her hands, already jumping to the next subject. "A makeover. Wouldn't you like that?"

"What's wrong with the way I look now?" Carissa asked defensively.

"Nothing, sweetheart. I think you're beautiful. I just thought that you'd want to try a *new* look."

The waiter reappeared with their drinks, allowing Carissa time to cool down. At this rate, she doubted if she would survive this visit.

"Besides, sweetheart. A woman should look her best at all times."

"You're starting to give me a complex."

"I mean it, Risa. When was the last time you were on a date? And I don't mean a business date. I mean a *real* date."

"I don't have time for a relationship right now. Hell, I'm practically married to Cartel Enterprises."

Helena shuddered. "What a dreadful marriage."

"It's not that bad. There's a lot of satisfaction being president of a successful company. I mean, there are plenty of women who'd love to be in my shoes."

"I can't think of a single person," Helena cut in. "What about success as a woman? Don't you ever dream of settling down and raising your two point five children?"

"What on earth is half a kid?"

Her aunt gave her a stern look. "You know what I mean. You've already confessed to being tired of the rat race of corporate America. Now you're trying to recant and tell me how much you love the business."

"Okay, so it's more like a love-hate relationship." Carissa shrugged. "I mean there are days I'm proud of all the things I've accomplished."

"And you should be. I have to admit, I didn't think that you'd last this long. But I miss my old Risa. The one that wanted to be a dancer."

Carissa laughed at that. "Trust me. My dancing days are long gone."

Helena watched her intently. "Don't you ever wonder what could have been?"

"Living in the land of 'what ifs' can drive a person insane. You, of all people, should know that."

"Now what is that supposed to mean?" Helena asked indignantly.

"Six marriages?" Carissa whispered above her

drink. "I love you dearly, but do you really think that you're the one to counsel me about marital bliss?"

"Cheap shot."

"Be that as it may, I'm right."

Helena's smile became forced. "All right. So I may not have been exactly successful in the marriage arena. But one of these days I plan on changing that."

"By painting every town you visit red?"

"It's better than cozying up to a cold laptop every night and suppressing my dreams."

Carissa leaned back in her chair and stared at her aunt. "Are we fighting?"

"It wasn't my intention." Helena took a sip of her margarita and, once again, reined in her temper. "I just want to see you happy. Is that too much to ask?"

For the first time that night, Carissa's smile was genuine. "No. It's not too much to ask."

In the next instant, Carissa's heart stopped at the sound of a familiar voice.

"Carissa?"

Both women turned and looked up into the handsome features of Nathan Edwards.

Chapter 13

"Nathan?" Carissa questioned in a voice that she didn't recognize. "What are you doing here?"

"Believe it or not, I'm actually going to eat a meal. I decided to take your advice and wean myself of coffee."

Helena cleared her throat.

"Oh, I'm sorry. Aunt Helena, I'd like for you to meet Nathan *Edwards*. Nathan, this is my aunt Helena."

"It's a pleasure to meet you." His head descended to kiss the back of her aunt's hand.

"What a charmer." Helena's eyes sparkled with delight. She lowered her hand and looked around him. "Are you here alone?"

"Actually, it seems I've been stood up. My stepfather left a message with the host that he'd been called away on business."

"I can't imagine anyone standing you up." Helena flirted with expertise.

Carissa's gaze shot to her aunt as her brows heightened. The woman was shameless.

"Well, you're more than welcome to join us. I'm sure Risa won't mind."

Carissa sent a swift kick to Helena's shin.

"Ouch."

"Risa?"

Carissa cringed. But when his dark gaze centered on her, her pulse rose.

"I like it," he said. "It suits you."

She returned his smile, yet felt too embarrassed to respond.

"Well, it does appear that I'm all dressed up with nowhere to go. And I am famished."

"Then that settles it," Helena declared. "You'll have dinner with us, right, Risa?"

Carissa's mouth fell. This was a train wreck waiting to happen. Helena and Nathan waited for her to speak.

"I'd love it if you could join us," she finally managed to respond.

"Great." Helena's smile brightened.

Nathan took a vacant seat. "It looks like we ended up having dinner together after all."

"Well, I hope you don't mind my chaperoning." Helena forced herself into the conversation.

"Not at all." Nathan returned his attention to her.

"I'm dining with two beautiful women instead of one. What man can ask for more?"

"You are adorable." Helena edged her chair closer.

Carissa watched her aunt's outrageous tactics, surprised by the instant pool of jealousy swirling in the pit of her stomach.

Helena reached out to pat Nathan's hand. "Risa told me about what happened with your father. I'm truly sorry."

"Thank you." He turned back toward Carissa. "Except for our rocky introduction, your niece has been a great shoulder to cry on."

Another wave of embarrassment darkened Carissa's face.

"My father is a lucky man to have you in his life."

"Come again?" Helena's eyes widened, then darted between the couple.

"Please, don't mention it. I feel honor-bound to visit him while he's in the hospital."

"Sir, can I get you anything to drink?"

While Nathan was distracted placing his drink order, Helena passed Carissa a stern look as she mouthed the words, "What's going on?"

"Well, ladies. Have we decided on what to order?" Nathan asked before Carissa could answer her aunt.

The waiter stood waiting.

"I have," Carissa lied, then called out the first thing her eyes landed on in the menu.

"Why is everything served with grits?" Helena inquired, surprised.

"I guess it's a Southern thing." Nathan laughed, then placed his order.

After they'd made their orders, Carissa was relieved that the conversation shifted to Nathan and his career as a photographer. She listened, fascinated, as he told stories of his travels abroad.

Then Helena took the wheel, and within five minutes, she wheedled out of him that the man wasn't involved in a serious relationship, he was financially secure, and he had no children. Carissa was impressed, but suspected that any moment her aunt was going to request references. She had spent a whole night talking to the man, and had come up empty.

Dinner arrived and Nathan's animated stories continued. Carissa was soon imagining herself in the wilds of Africa, or the mystic beauty of India. Better yet, what would those places be like with a man like him?

As he talked, she couldn't help but study his features. It didn't seem right that a man possessed such long curly lashes. And that smile. The man could easily be a poster ad for Colgate.

"Well, enough about me. I must be boring you ladies." He did manage to look embarrassed at his conclusion.

"Not at all," Helena reassured him. "I swear if I were a few years younger, I'd try my best to convince you to take me on one of your wild adventures."

A few years? Carissa frowned.

"I would be more than happy to take you anytime you like," he boasted.

Jealousy reared its ugly head and Carissa struggled to pacify the demon. Why didn't she inherit her aunt's flirtatious nature? In fact, she downright felt like the ugly goose sitting next to Helena. Maybe she should reconsider that makeover.

"You know, Risa knows quite a bit about modeling," Helena bragged.

"Let's not talk about that right now," Carissa warned. She would absolutely die if her aunt started regaling Nathan about her short modeling stint when she was a toddler.

"Is that right? I had a feeling you were a model. I bet the camera just loves you." His gaze slid over her features. "I know I would love to photograph you."

Helena cleared her voice. "I think I need to powder my nose. Risa, do you mind coming with me?"

Carissa blinked to break the hypnotic spell of his eyes. "Uh, yes. Of course. Will you excuse us?"

"Sure." He stood as they left the table.

Seconds later, Helena had her cornered in the restroom. "That man is crazy about you. You'd be a fool to toss that fish back in the pond."

"Cut me a break, Auntie. The man thinks I'm involved with his father. Nurse Anne probably told him I'm Travis's fiancée."

"Then tell him the truth. I'm sure he'll understand that you had to lie about your relationship in order to visit his father."

"Oh, really?" Carissa crossed her arms. "Do you

also propose that I tell him that I'm the reason his father is lying in the hospital in the first place?"

Helena bit her lip.

"I didn't think so. Like I told you before, the best thing for me to do is steer clear of him. I shouldn't be dining with him, pretending to be someone I'm not."

"But the man is obviously fond of you. Surely—"

"Trust me, Auntie. I know what I'm doing on this. After tonight, I have no plans on ever seeing that man again."

Nathan stood and pulled out their chairs when they returned.

"I hope we didn't keep you waiting too long," Helena said, taking her seat.

"Of course not. I was afraid I had actually chased you ladies off. I tend to get a little carried away when I start talking about my work."

"Don't be silly. We've enjoyed your company."

He glanced toward Carissa, puzzled by her tight smile. Something was wrong. The group fell silent and retreated to their own private thoughts.

"You know, there is something I would love to show you," Helena exclaimed, startling Nathan at the sudden outburst.

"Risa, can I see your car keys? I want to get something from the car."

"What?" Carissa eyes her suspiciously.

"It's a surprise."

Carissa's eyes narrowed.

"Please? I promise it's nothing that would embarrass you."

Nathan wasn't sure of what was going on, but he sensed Helena was up to something.

Reluctantly, Carissa retrieved the keys from her purse.

"Thank you. I'll be right back." She stood, then winked at him as she strode from the table.

She's definitely up to something, he confirmed to himself.

Once they were alone, Nathan leaned forward. "I hope I haven't done something to upset you. I'll feel terrible if you really didn't want me to join you. I swear I don't make a habit of imposing on people."

His apologetic look made her feel ashamed of her behavior. But heaven knew she couldn't help it. Whenever the man was near, she went from a strong, independent woman to an insecure, jealousy-prone idiot. "There's really no need for you to apologize. It's me. I just really had a rough day. I'm glad you joined us for dinner."

Nathan had his doubts.

"Really," she added, covering his hand for emphasis. But the moment her hand made contact, her heart skipped a beat.

His gaze lowered. Then he placed his free hand atop hers.

She felt dizzy at the exquisite feel of his caress.

How was it possible that such large hands could feel so soft?

When his gaze returned to her face, his brows were heightened with curiosity. "No engagement ring?"

Chapter 14

"Let me explain," Carissa began, but she couldn't think of a single lie to bail her out. "I told the hospital I was engaged to your father because it was the only way they would let me see him."

Nathan released her hand. "So you lied?"

Her brows rose at the undeniable anger laced in his voice. "I lied to the *hospital* about my relationship. I have to admit I was a little concerned when none of his family members had shown up," she added defensively. It was partly true, she reasoned with herself.

Contrite, he nodded. "I guess I can understand that."

"You guess?" she repeated. Her sudden anger surprised her. All thoughts of finishing her confession flew out the window. "You know, Mr. Edwards. I changed my mind. I think this was a mistake. I have no intentions of sitting here while you cast judgment—"

"Judgment?" he thundered incredulously. Then, as if he realized what he'd done, he lowered his voice. "Is that what you think I'm doing?"

"Well, aren't you?"

"Excuse me, ma'am?" the waiter interrupted. "This was left for you." He handed her a folded note.

Jaws clenched, she accepted the note. She gazed over the words, then shook her head in disbelief. "I'm going to kill her."

"Let me guess." Nathan leaned back with a knowing smile. "She took off."

"You have to excuse my aunt. She loves practical jokes."

"Or perhaps playing matchmaker?"

"I'll take a cab," Carissa declared, then waved for the waiter. "Check, please."

"Nonsense. I'll take you home."

"What—so we can continue arguing in the car?"

"How about if we called a truce," he offered. But for some odd reason he enjoyed arguing with her. He liked when her face flushed and her eyes lit up. He had a feeling the woman had engaged and won quite a few battles in her lifetime.

"I was expecting something more like an apology." She crossed her arms and patiently drummed her fingers.

Oh, yes, he thought, the woman knew how to get what she wanted. And lucky for her, he was in the mood to accommodate her. "You have my sincerest apologies, Ms. Carnes."

She looked away.

"It wasn't my intention to sound like I was in any way judging you." When she visibly relaxed, he went on to explain. "I just left a relationship where…" He waved the speech off. "It's not important."

She remained quiet, not sure of what to say. When the check arrived, she reached for her purse.

"Don't even think about it." Nathan retrieved his wallet. "No woman pays for a meal around me."

"Sounds chauvinistic."

"I thought I was being romantic."

Their gazes deepened with their light banter. However, Carissa was never one to remain speechless for long. "A girl could get the impression that you're on the rebound."

"Hardly." He turned serious again. "I've had time to get over it."

"That bad?"

"Worse." He gripped his drink. "In retrospect, I guess I should have seen it coming."

Her keen gaze caught the flicker of pain that crossed his features as he lifted the glass. She was sorry she had brought up the subject.

"Honesty is one of the most important ingredients in a relationship," he said thoughtfully. "That and communication. India and I had neither."

Pretty name, she thought.

Nathan laughed and shook his head. "I'm doing it again."

"Doing what?"

"Treating you like you're my shrink or something. Of course, this would never happen if you weren't such a good listener."

This time she laughed. "It's okay. Believe it or not, I rather enjoy our little talks."

"You're an interesting woman, Ms. Carnes. I'll give you that."

She shrugged. "I've been called worse."

"I find that hard to believe."

Playfully her eyes narrowed, unable to tell whether he was joking. "Well, don't. I've been told plenty of times I've inherited my father's temper as well as his nose for business."

"Ah, an ill-tempered fashion model. Now that's something you don't hear about every day."

"Ha. I'm no model."

He frowned. "But your aunt said—"

"She was referring to when I was three years old." Carissa shook her head. "I did a few print ads and that's about it."

"I bet you were a beautiful baby."

Carissa's body grew warm. "Do you always say the right thing at the right time?"

"No. I think I'm just on a roll." He puffed out his chest, then grinned at her sudden burst of laughter. *She's wonderful,* he thought. He wanted to talk to her

for hours again, listen to her thoughts about everything that kept him lying awake at night.

"Have you decided how long you're staying in
town?" she asked, averting her gaze.

He shrugged. "I keep changing my mind every ten
minutes. I know I should stay. Especially now since
I'm starting to suspect foul play."

Her heart dropped. "Foul play? What do you
mean?"

"I can't put my finger on it." He shrugged, then met
her gaze again. "How did *you* find out what happened?"

Think. Think. "I, uh, received a call."

"Was it from a Ms. Townsend?"

She swallowed, then forced her best poker face. "I
believe so. Why?"

"She contacted me, too. Today, I decided to find
out a little more about what led up to his heart attack.
So I gave her a call, then went by to see her."

"What did she say?" she asked cautiously.

"It's not what she said that's bothering me."

"No?"

"It's what she wouldn't say. I got the impression
she was hiding something."

Carissa didn't dare say anything.

"I don't know." He shrugged out of his reverie.
"Maybe I'm imagining things."

"I need another drink. Waiter."

Nathan frowned. "Is there something wrong?"

"No. I'm just thirsty." She placed her order and the
waited adjusted their check before strolling off.

"I get the impression that if we were to have a contest you could drink me under the table."

"You're damn right."

He laughed. "I guess there's an upside to this. At this rate, I'll have to peel you off me by the end of the night."

"You're daydreaming again."

"Am I?" His brows wiggled back at her. "Now that I know you're available the rules have changed."

Another rush of heat swept over her. There was no mistaking his meaning. "Just because I'm not engaged to your father doesn't mean that I'm available."

"Good point. Are you involved with anyone?"

"That's none of your business."

He studied her. "Then I'm going to pretend that you're not. Maybe even pretend that we're actually on our first date."

Smiling, she shook her head. "Do you always just go after what you want?"

"Relentlessly."

"That's another thing we have in common." Her expression sobered when their eyes met again. "But the reality is that we've known each other only two days—two very unusual days. It's hardly the makings of a relationship."

He nodded as if he were processing this information. "Well, how about a night of unbridled passion?"

"What?" Her eyes widened.

Nathan's serious mask crumbled as his shoulders shook with mirth. "Relax. I was just joking."

She relaxed.

"I can wait another two days."

When her eyes narrowed, his amusement deepened.

"You may find this hard to believe, Mr. Edwards, but I'm not attracted to you," she lied.

Nathan covered his heart with his hands. "Ouch. You really know how to hurt a man."

She finally laughed. "You're something else."

"I've been told that before."

"No doubt from your ex." She clamped her jaws shut, regretting her quick retort.

"Ah. Is that jealousy I hear?"

"No."

He studied her again, unable to break her perfect poker face. "You're a tough one to figure out."

"You're right. And I aim to stay that way."

Much later, the couple's conversation returned to more serious matters. But this time, it was Carissa's turn on the psychiatrist's couch.

"So you never went to see him before he died?" Nathan asked, sullen.

She nearly choked on her answer. "No."

"If you had to do it all over again?"

"In a heartbeat." She chewed her bottom lip. "I'm not happy at all about how things have turned out." Her voice trailed off.

"I'm sorry." He enclosed her hands in his and caressed the tips of her fingers. She was struck by how small hers seemed.

"It's okay. I have no one to blame but myself. After his death, I was consumed with the need to make him proud of me. All my accomplishments have left me hollow because I don't like what I've become."

"What is it that you do?"

Ruin people's lives. "I just help run a small family business," she whispered.

He squeezed her hand. "The way you were talking I was beginning to think that you worked for the mob."

She smiled. "No. It's nothing that drastic." She looked down at their hands. "But you need to know that guilt is a very powerful thing. That's why I say if there's any way for you to make peace with your father, grab hold of it with both hands and don't you dare let go."

Carissa's words echoed in Nathan's head as he drove her home. He was already experiencing the power of his guilty conscience. Shortly after he'd graduated from college, he'd received a letter from Travis saying how much he wanted to see him again. But Nathan had been astonished by the man's audacity. He remembered laughing while he tore up the letter, then remembered later nursing his guilt over a bottle of tequila.

"Take a right at the corner," Carissa instructed from the passenger seat of his rented Bronco.

"It's this building right here."

Nathan looked up at the luxury high-rise. "You live here?"

She looked flustered. "Yeah. It's really not as expensive as it looks." She shrugged.

Was she kidding? He knew exactly how much it cost to live in this area of town. "Are you sure you don't work for the mob?"

She laughed. "I really appreciate your bringing me home. After I wring my aunt's neck, I'm sure it will never happen again."

He parked inside the garage.

"You know it's not necessary for you to walk me to the door."

"Nonsense. I wouldn't be a gentleman if I didn't escort you safely home."

She started to protest again, but the look on his face told her she was wasting her breath.

When they stepped from the elevator, Nathan was immediately impressed by the subtle elegance that greeted him. He glanced down at his simple black jeans and snug cotton turtleneck and felt under-dressed. "Nice place."

"Thank you," she said uneasily. She thought the walk to her suite seemed unbelievably long. When her front door came into view, she exhaled. "Here we are." She tested the knob and was relieved her aunt hadn't locked her out.

"Then I guess this is good night?"

"It looks that way." She glanced at her watch. "I'd invite you in for a nightcap, but it's pretty late."

He looked at the time. "Three o'clock. I'm sorry I kept you past curfew, but I really enjoyed your company. You gave me a lot to think about."

"I hope I was able to help."

"You were."

They fell silent. Neither knew how to end the evening.

"Good night, Risa." He leaned forward and tipped her chin up with his fingers and placed a tender kiss against her lips.

A sweet sensation pooled within her body, making it impossible for her to hold on to a clear thought. When he pulled away, her quick intake of air burned her lungs. "Good night," she managed to whisper.

He smiled, then turned and walked away.

Carissa watched him as he moved down the hallway and knew that she had just made a horrible mistake. Turning, she entered her penthouse, then slumped behind the closed door. She was playing with fire and she had no idea how she was going to put out the flames Nathan Edwards had ignited.

Chapter 15

Nathan didn't drive home. Despite the late hour, he returned to Northside Hospital. Carissa had given him a lot to think about. Maybe the past was exactly where it needed to be, in the past. *Easier said than done,* he thought.

The sorrow that seemed to possess her when she spoke of her father troubled him. Hell, he felt downright sorry for her. Yet it was a path he was in danger of following. He knew what he needed to do, but it still wasn't easy.

As he traveled through the empty hallways, he tried to figure out a way to bury years of heartache. And he wondered if he was capable of forgiving. He'd always viewed things as black and white. There was no such thing as a gray area. It was probably why he was so hard on people, including India.

When he arrived in the ICU, Nurse Anne greeted him with a smile. In their brief conversation, he learned that there was no change in his father's condition. Dr. Peterson warned him that there was a possibility of his father remaining in a coma for years. Nathan prayed that wasn't how this Shakespearean tragedy would end.

Moments later, he sat beside Travis's bed, staring at his still form. Had his father thought of him often over the past thirty years? Had he regretted his decision to walk out on him? Nathan hoped so.

Guilt can be a very powerful thing. Carissa's voice floated through his head. He exhaled and leaned forward to take Travis's hand. It was still cold.

"This isn't easy for me," he said above the lump in the center of his throat. "I want you to wake up. I know there's nothing, yet everything, between us. But I don't want to go through life with any more regrets. I can only hope that you feel the same way."

Tears slid from Nathan's eyes with his heartfelt confession. "It took a friend of yours to help me figure all this out. And I'm very grateful to her." He smiled. "Who knows—maybe one day I'll learn what happened when you returned from Vietnam."

Travis's eyes moved behind his closed lids while his mind drifted back in time…

Chicago, May 18, 1972

Travis glanced at his watch and exhaled in frustration. Maybe Val had gotten lost, he reasoned. In the back of his mind, he doubted it. For some time, he couldn't shake this sense of impending doom. He didn't know where this feeling came from—all he knew was that it grew stronger by the minute.

In his duffel bag, he carried every letter, picture and gift she had sent during the war. They were items he would always treasure. But right now, he was anxious to see his family, to compare his memory with the real thing.

Travis turned to the sound of an approaching car, then shielded his eyes from the glaring sun. Once again, he was disappointed with the make and model.

He looked at his watch again, his anxiety slowly turning into fear.

"Hey, buddy. Are you just going to stand there all day or are you going to get in?"

Travis's head jerked up at the familiar voice and an instant grin covered his face. "Smokey! I'll be damned. What the hell are you doing here?" He grabbed his belongings and headed to the car.

"Doing you a favor. If you didn't buy Val that jalopy, she would have been here to pick you up."

Relief swelled in Travis's chest as he jerked the door open and tossed his things into the backseat. "If you think that this junker of yours is more reliable, then you need to get your head examined." He climbed into the passenger seat.

"I'm here, aren't I?"

"Great. Now let's see if we can make it back."

The men slapped each other's backs and laughed. During the drive home, Travis gazed out the window, admiring his hometown and the welcoming landscape. "I miss this place," he whispered.

Smokey chuckled. "Spoken like a man coming back from a war. I'd imagine anything would look good to you right now."

"You don't know how right you are, my friend," Travis agreed. "But I have to admit, I've learned a lot about myself—about the world."

"I wouldn't doubt it. Especially after all you've been through." Smokey glanced in his direction. "Val told me you took one in the gut a while back."

"Man, I took a lot of things. I've got scars in places I'd be ashamed to show my own mother."

"Then definitely don't show me. I'll just take your word for it."

"Deal."

For a while, the men rode in silence before Smokey added, "I'm glad you've made it back."

Travis turned and met his direct gaze. "Thanks. That's good to hear."

A few minutes later, Smokey passed his neighborhood. "Where are we going?"

"To your apartment."

"Apartment? What happened to the house?"

Their astonished gazes locked.

"She didn't tell you?"

"Tell me what?"

"With all due respect, buddy, I think I need to let her tell you."

That nagging feeling returned, and this time Travis knew better than to shrug it off.

The apartment was small—too small. Travis forced a brave face. Maybe Val fell on hard times and had to sell the house. Yet he wondered why she hadn't mentioned it in her letters. None of that mattered, he told himself. He was back home and would fix everything.

The moment he opened the door, six-year-old Nathan sprinted toward him. "Daddy, Daddy."

Travis dropped his bags and swept his son high into the air. "Hey! Did ya miss me?"

"Yeah!" Nathan laughed as his father spun him around in a circle.

"Welcome home." Val's soft voice somehow penetrated the father and son reunion. All eyes turned toward her.

Travis drew in a sharp breath. "My God."

"Mommy, you look pretty," Nathan exclaimed when his father lowered him to the floor.

She stood in the entranceway with her tightly coiled hair in a neat Afro. Her clear chestnut complexion glowed, and when she smiled, the room lit up.

He moved toward her, his gaze soaking in every detail. "It's been a long time," he whispered.

"Too long." She rushed into his open arms, their lips instantly locking in an inferno of passion.

"I guess you two would like to be alone."

The couple separated as Travis turned, laughing at his best friend. "I'd forgotten you were still here."

"I see you weren't the only one." Smokey's gaze landed on Val briefly, then he held his arms out to Nathan. "Come and tell your uncle Smokey goodbye."

Nathan happily did as he was instructed. "Aren't you going to stay for dinner tonight?"

"Nah, not tonight. I'll try and stop by and see ya tomorrow."

Travis, with his arm looped around his wife, walked over to his best friend. "Thanks, man. I really appreciate your coming to pick me up." He tightened his embrace. "And I want to thank you for looking after my little family. It looks like you did a terrific job." He held out his free hand.

Smokey's smile suddenly appeared tight and forced, Travis noted fleetingly as his friend accepted his hand in a tight handshake.

"It was my pleasure."

An awkward silence encircled the small group before Smokey spoke again. "I'll catch you guys later." He put Nathan down and left the apartment, the door slamming slightly behind him.

Puzzled, Travis stood looking at the door. "Did I miss something?"

"I'm sure it's nothing," Val reassured him. She reached up and gently turned his face toward her. *"Are you hungry? I made your favorite dish."*

He smiled. *"I'm hungry, but trust me, it isn't for food."*

"Behave. Don't forget your son is still in the room," she whispered. *"But I think I can help you satisfy your hunger a little later."*

Days later, Travis returned home from the bank, disgusted that he had been unable to get a loan. As it had turned out, Val had lost her job nearly a year ago when the county had rezoned their old area and a few schools were closed. Since that time, she and Nathan had been surviving off welfare.

The army had already informed him that there would be a delay in his receiving his disability pay. But what bothered him most was the five-thousand-dollar loan Val accepted from Smokey. He didn't know why the transaction bothered him. He'd been friends with Smokey since grade school. He should have been grateful that Smokey had helped his family. But he wasn't.

When he closed the front door, his hackles stood at attention. His ears perked up at the explosive argument coming from the kitchen.

"What do you expect me to do?" Smokey barked. *"I can't sit by and watch you with him. It's killing me. I thought that I could let you go because I love you and Nathan. I love Travis. We're like brothers."*

An Important Message from the Publisher

Dear Reader,

Because you've chosen to read one of our fine novels, I'd like to say "thank you"! And, as a special way to say thank you, I'm offering to send you two more Kimani™ Romance novels and two surprise gifts – absolutely FREE! These books will keep it real with true-to-life African American characters that turn up the heat and sizzle with passion.

Please enjoy the free books and gifts with our compliments...

Glenda Howard

For Kimani Press

Peel off Seal and Place Inside...

FREE GIFTS
EDITOR'S SEAL
THANK YOU

YES! I have placed my

Editor's "thank you" Free Gifts seal in the space provided at right. Please send me 2 FREE books, and my 2 FREE Mystery Gifts. I understand that I am under no obligation to purchase anything further, as explained on the back of this card.

About how many NEW paperback fiction books have you purchased in the past 3 months?

❏ 0-2
EZQE

❏ 3-6
EZQQ

❏ 7 or more
EZQ2

168/368 XDL

FIRST NAME	LAST NAME

ADDRESS

APT.#	CITY

STATE/PROV.	ZIP/POSTAL CODE

Thank You!

BUSINESS REPLY MAIL

FIRST-CLASS MAIL   PERMIT NO. 717   BUFFALO, NY

POSTAGE WILL BE PAID BY ADDRESSEE

THE READER SERVICE
PO BOX 1867
BUFFALO NY 14240-9952

NO POSTAGE
NECESSARY
IF MAILED
IN THE
UNITED STATES

Val muffled her sobs when her hands covered her face. "Don't do this to us, Smokey. I've told you that I love my husband. What happened between us…"

Her sentence trailed off when she removed her hands and saw Travis standing just inches behind Smokey. "Oh, my God."

Startled, Smokey jerked around. "Travis."

Chapter 16

Carissa couldn't sleep. Every time she closed her eyes, Nathan's dark, soulful eyes stared back at her. Her heartbeat accelerated and her body grew warm as she realized that she was falling hard. It was the worst thing that could have happened.

Minutes later, she gave up on sleep and headed for the kitchen. She jerked open the refrigerator door and stared blankly inside. What the hell was she doing? Food was the last thing she wanted. She slammed the door and went over to the dining-room table.

As if on cue, the front door swept open and a singing Helena sauntered into the penthouse.

Carissa glanced at her watch. "It's five in the morning."

Helena turned toward her voice. "Good. That means it's still early." She spun around and danced with an imaginary partner. "Girl, I love this town."

"Let me guess. You found your Black Chippendale dancers."

"Honey, I discovered paradise. I swear if I was just a few years younger I would have snagged one of those young whippersnappers."

"You ought to be ashamed of yourself."

Helena danced toward Carissa. "Don't start raining on my parade just because I know how to have a good time. Let me guess, you had the handsome hunk bring you home by nine-thirty."

"No. I just made it in a couple of hours ago. And speaking of which, you had some nerve just dumping me like that. What were you thinking? I'd just explained why I needed to avoid the man."

Helena waved off her niece's argument. "I know if I were you, that man would be the last person I'd avoid."

"Will you please be serious for a moment. I'm trying to prevent this from blowing up in my face and you're sitting there trying to play matchmaker."

"Risa, love isn't a deadly disease. Stop trying to do everything to make yourself undesirable." Helena pulled the hair band from Carissa's head. Thick, full curls tumbled to her shoulders. "You're beautiful."

Carissa stood, shaking her head. "Sometimes I wonder if we're even from the same planet, let alone share the same genes."

Her aunt crossed her arms. "Are you trying to tell me that there aren't nights when you lie awake craving the touch of a soul mate, a man who understands you, someone who is an extension of yourself?"

Carissa fell silent.

"No?" Helena went on. "How about a man who makes you feel safe whenever you're in his arms, or has a way of making you feel beautiful just by looking at you." Helena shook her head. "If you can look me in the eyes and tell me that you've never craved any of those things, then I agree, we *are* from two different planets."

Carissa's shoulders sagged in defeat. "Of course I want those things. But this is the wrong time, the wrong guy."

"How do you know? I saw the way he looks at you. I bet he can sketch you with his eyes closed. Hell, after six marriages, I can tell you that none of my husbands looked at me like that."

"You're imagining things."

"No. You're in denial and about to throw away a chance of a lifetime."

Helena spun on her heels and left Carissa to think on what she'd said.

Carissa watched her departure with a growing sense of hopelessness. How her aunt continued to look at life through rose-colored glasses was beyond her. Sure there were a few things she liked about Nathan other than that he was easy on the eyes.

His complex personality intrigued her. When he talked about his work, she heard his passion and love for his art.

Before long, Carissa found herself wondering what really ended his engagement to India. The woman's name soured in her mouth. No doubt she was a knockout with legs up to her neck.

She sat at the table, depressed. Why in the hell did she care who the man dated—or what kind of woman he preferred? Since he was a photographer, she had no trouble believing he preferred the model type. She stood and went over to a mirror hanging in the living room and took a good look at herself.

She posed playfully, assessing her appearance. *I'm all right,* she concluded, but she was unhappy that there wasn't anything that stood out about her features—other than her hair.

Running her fingers through the thick mass, she watched how her natural curls framed her face and enhanced the shape of her eyes.

"See, I told you you were beautiful."

Carissa jumped at the sound of her aunt's voice. "Don't you ever sleep? I thought you'd gone to bed."

Helena waved her off. "I told you, it's still early. Have you thought more about what I said?"

"I admit that I would love to find a special someone and eventually go on to raise a family." She exhaled and crossed her arms. "But like I said, it's the wrong time and the wrong man."

Nathan woke to a ringing phone. "Hello."

"Ah, so you're alive."

"Smokey?" Nathan sat up and glanced around. "What time is it?"

"Six-thirty."

"A.M.?"

He laughed. "I take it you had another all-nighter at the hospital."

"Yes and no. What happened to you last night? I thought we were going to have dinner."

"I'm sorry. I was called away. I left you a message at the door. You didn't get it?"

"Yeah, I got it. It's just that I've never been stood up before. Lucky for me, I ran into Dad's—I mean Travis's friend from the hospital. I had dinner with her."

There was a slight pause over the line before Smokey said, "I see."

Nathan heard the hurt in his voice and mentally kicked himself. "Are you sure you're all right with all of this? I mean, I want you to understand why—"

"Look, son. You don't owe me any explanations. If this is important to you, then it's important to me."

"You don't know how much I appreciate hearing that." Nathan smiled against the phone. "It's also important to me that you know that I'm not looking to replace you."

"I know that."

When Smokey exhaled, it sounded more like a sigh of relief to Nathan.

"So this is the same lady you were telling me about the other day?"

"Yeah. It turns out that she's *not* engaged to Travis. She only told the hospital that in order to be able to see my father."

"She sounds resourceful."

"Among other things. I can't blame her, really. I probably would have done the same thing if I were in her position."

"Mr. Honesty is condoning a lie? This woman really must be something."

"It's not that. It just seems that my father doesn't have too many friends. Hell, she probably thought I wasn't coming to see him either. Seems to me she's the only friend Travis has."

"Sounds like you're still interested."

Nathan's smile widened. "I don't know what I am, to tell you the truth. But it helps that she's been through a similar situation with her father. She's given me a lot to think about."

"She's starting to intrigue me, too. What did you say this Angel of Mercy's name was?"

"Carissa Carnes."

"Carnes?"

"Yes? Do you know her?"

"N-no. Not a Carissa Carnes, but it's not like your father and I traveled in the same circles."

Nathan nodded, but he sensed there was something Smokey wasn't telling him.

Chapter 17

Carissa's heartbeat pounded in her ears as she jogged up an inclining hill around the base of Stone Mountain. She had long tuned out the music playing through the headset of her CD player, and she struggled to make sense of the steady stream of conflicting thoughts running through her head.

For the past week, she'd buried herself in her work. However, the attempt did little to ease her guilty conscience. In fact, it seemed to make matters worse. In an effort to avoid any further confrontations with clients or competitors, she had Liz cancel a month's worth of meetings. It was illogical, she realized, but she couldn't help how she felt. Just as she couldn't help how her mind kept returning to Nathan Edwards's haunting eyes.

She picked up her pace and even increased the volume on her CD player. But when his image persisted, the music was once again forgotten. She'd learned from the nurses the amount of time Nathan spent with his father. Again she envied his possible second chance.

But what would you say if you did have a second chance with your father? Carissa's mind drew a blank. After she traveled another mile, she stopped and shook her head. She had no idea what she would have said or done differently.

Closing her eyes, she tilted her head up toward the sky, relishing the sun's warmth as she grabbed the small water bottle strapped to her hip.

She also didn't know how much longer she could avoid running into Nathan at Cartel Enterprises. The man came every day wanting to talk to C. J. Cartel. Yesterday, she had hidden in the restroom for more than two hours. Something had to give.

She removed her headset just when a loud masculine voice shouted her name close by. She jumped, then pivoted with her hand over her heart.

Nathan's unexpected appearance startled her.

He jogged to a stop beside her. "I thought I'd never catch up with you."

When he flashed her a brief smile, for a shocking moment her legs weakened. "What are you doing here?"

"George and I decided to have our morning run up here." He nodded to a handsome German shepherd panting happily at his side.

At first glance at the dog's adorable expression, she couldn't help but kneel down and run her hands along the dog's soft coat.

"Ah, don't tell me you're a dog lover as well?"

"Only if they love me back." She smiled as she looked up and held his gaze.

"Well, George and I are trying to enjoy our short time together. He leaves tomorrow with my assistant."

An awkward silence passed before she gathered her composure and stood. "How are you doing?" seemed like the only safe thing to ask.

"I'm doing well. All things considered." His smile never faltered, yet she saw something flicker in his eyes, and she wondered how she should reach out to him. But she was the last person in the world who knew how to reach out to people.

"I've missed seeing you at the hospital," he said, continuing to hold her gaze. "I hope I didn't run you off."

"No, not at all. It's just that I've been sort of busy," she stammered with the excuse and actually felt a rush of heat burn her face.

"I see." He leaned down and scratched behind George's ear. "Well, I felt guilty just the same. I realize I can come on a bit strong at times—"

"No. Really, it wasn't you. I just felt like I was intruding on your time with your father. I don't belong there."

"That's nonsense." He shrugged off her excuse. "It's apparent to me that my father's well-being means a lot to you. And I know about your daily calls to the hospital. Nurse Anne speaks highly of you."

Carissa's mouth opened in surprise as she struggled to come up with a response.

"It's okay," Nathan added. "I really do understand."

"You couldn't possibly." She shook her head. "I'm sorry. There's no excuse for the way I've behaved toward you. But trust me when I say that my not coming to the hospital has very little to do with you and everything to do with my relationship with your father."

"I see." Disappointment flashed across his handsome features, but he quickly added, "I know this may sound strange coming from me, especially when you consider the history between me and my father, but I think he needs you right now."

"You don't understand," she persisted.

"Maybe not. All I know is you seem to be one of the few friends he has right now. I suppose my father is a bit of a loner. He's going to need our prayers to get through this. If you want, I can arrange my visits so that I'm not there when you come."

Carissa blinked. "That won't be necessary. I rather enjoyed your company. I think I can arrange to come by this afternoon to check on Edwards."

Nathan's brows arched. "You call him by his last name?"

Damn. "N-no. I meant Travis. I—I wasn't thinking."

He smiled. "If I didn't know any better, I'd swear I made you nervous."

Her mouth opened in protest, and he held up a hand to stop any quick retort.

"Relax. It was a joke. I hope this means I'll see you later this afternoon. Maybe then I'll be able to convince you to go on a second date." He flashed her another smile, then called to his companion. "Come on, George. I'm sure you'll get another chance to see the pretty lady."

Nathan winked and led George away, while Carissa tried to make sense of what had just happened.

Hours later, Carissa breezed into the office, hoping to pick up a few things without an incident. Liz wasn't at her desk as she rushed into her office, but Carissa froze in her tracks the moment she saw Colin Hunter sitting behind her desk.

"How in the hell did you get in here?" Carissa jabbed her fists against her hips.

"How isn't half as important as why." Colin smiled. "I thought that this would be the perfect time to celebrate."

"Celebrate?" She shook her head. "You obviously have no idea what I've been through in the past week. And just where have you been? I've been leaving messages all over the place for you."

He stood and with long, confident strides swallowed the space between them. "If you're referring to what happened with Edwards, I already know about it. It's a minor setback, but I don't see why we can't move on with our plans."

Incredulous, Carissa stared at him. "What?"

Colin shrugged. "Come on, Cartel. Like you always say, 'Business is business—it's never personal.'"

"What kind of rivalry do you have with this man? I never knew your competitiveness extended to wishing actual harm. Yes, business is business, but this is something else entirely." She kept her steady gaze leveled with his.

Colin turned and headed back toward the desk. "I'm sorry," he said over his shoulder. "But you're wrong." He faced her and leaned back against the desk. "There's no rivalry. I hardly know Edwards. I'm anxious to get this project under way. You haven't changed your mind, have you?"

Had she? "I haven't had time to decide what I'm going to do about anything. And there's no real need to address the issue now."

"I see." He studied her. "You're not going soft on me, are you, Cartel?"

When she didn't answer, he added, "I thought I'd never see the day."

Carissa bit back her anger. "Okay. So you've discovered I'm human—sue me. Now, if you don't mind, the last time I checked, this was still my office."

"I can take a hint." He headed for the door. "But think about it. With Edwards temporarily out of the picture, we can get things done faster than we had planned."

Carissa shook her head. "You mean faster than *you* had planned."

A strained silence filled the room as Colin's usual

stony features cracked. "I thought we were in this together."

"Don't take it personally. It's just business." Carissa's shoulders straightened. "I think maybe you should leave."

He stepped forward, then stopped. Suddenly, his whole demeanor changed. "You're right." His hands lowered to his sides. "I'm letting my ambitions take over and I apologize."

Her gaze narrowed.

"No hard feelings."

Whether it was a statement or a question, Carissa wasn't sure, nor did she care.

He smiled, but she couldn't force herself to return the gesture. Instead, she walked to the door and held it open.

His incredulous stare narrowed. "As you wish."

He glided past her. A question seemed to linger in his eyes, but she chose to ignore it. With a flick of her wrist, she slammed the door.

Chapter 18

Carissa worked late despite her promise to Nathan to stop by the hospital. Sure, she was concerned about his father's health, but masquerading as the man's fiancée with the staff, then convincing his son that she was a concerned *friend* was taking things too far.

What if Travis woke up and exposed her—then what? Leaning back against the chair, she wondered if she was dealing with a full deck. She shook her head. Who was she kidding? She wanted to see *Nathan*—plain and simple. The man monopolized her thoughts. In the week that she'd avoided him, she missed being with him and talking with him.

Yes, it was the wrong time and he was definitely the wrong man, but she'd be damned if she could help the way she felt. *This is crazy.* She grabbed her handbag. *I'll just go for thirty minutes and that's it,* she decided.

"I'll see you in the morning," she said to Liz, who was also getting ready to leave. A sniffle caught Carissa's attention. She stopped and turned back toward her secretary. "Liz, is there something wrong?"

Liz kept her head down and dabbed her eyes with a Kleenex. "Yeah, I'm fine."

Carissa frowned at the obvious lie. But when she thought about it, there was no reason Liz should confide in her. When was the last time she had inquired how her loyal secretary was doing?

"You don't look fine," Carissa said, moving toward her desk. "Is there anything I can help you with?"

Liz choked back a sob and shook her head.

Carissa's shoulders sagged. What did she expect? Liz stopped and dropped her belongings.

Carissa rushed around the desk and took the sobbing secretary into her arms. They clung to each other for a long time until Liz's heart-wrenching sobs subsided.

"I'm so sorry, Ms. Cartel. I—I just received some bad news and I— Actually, I thought that I was more prepared for this."

Carissa allowed her to pull away, but she stared, stupefied by her distraught secretary. She'd never seen Liz, the overly cheerful employee, in this condition. "Please tell me there is something I can do."

"N-no." Liz snatched another Kleenex from the

box. "It's my grandmother. I just got a call. She's passed away." She knelt to collect her belongings.

Carissa knelt to help her.

"I have to go and pick up Darius." Liz pressed her hand over her heart. "Oh, my God! He's going to be devastated."

"They were close?"

Liz nodded. "Very."

Tears stung Carissa's eyes. "I had no idea."

Liz's gaze flew to her employer. "I'm not surprised."

Carissa pulled back at the sharp retort, but she relaxed when Liz's features softened.

"Let's face it, Ms. Cartel. You've never expressed interest in what's going on in your employees' lives. If you had then you'd know that Mr. Duran's wife has been diagnosed with breast cancer, and that Mrs. Nelson has been absent because of a severe case of bronchitis."

"It's impossible for me to keep up with every *employee*," Carissa said, defending herself.

Liz shrugged. "You're right. Forgive me. I better go."

"Wait."

Liz stopped.

"You're right, too." Carissa exhaled. "I haven't expressed an interest in a lot of things. And I'm sorry. But I'm trying to change all of that. I'm truly sorry for the loss of your grandmother. If there's anything I can do, please don't hesitate to call me."

Liz's gaze searched hers. Then, as if she had read Carissa's sincerity, she smiled. "Thanks. I needed to hear that."

Carissa embraced her. "Now, you go on home. Take as much time off as you need." The women headed out of the office together.

When they parted ways outside the double glass doors, Carissa turned and rammed hard into a solid mass. But before she could fall backward, a pair of strong hands grabbed her.

"This must be my lucky day."

Carissa recognized the man's rich baritone as she pulled away. "I'm starting to believe you're following me." She removed her sunglasses.

"It's not a bad idea," Nathan responded with a wide smile. "Maybe then I'd know why you're leaving Cartel Enterprises. You're not fraternizing with the enemy, are you?"

The color drained from her face as she looked guiltily up at the building. "Uh, yes...I mean no." *Think. Think.* "Actually, I came to see if I could get in to see Cartel, but he's not in."

"Again?" Nathan's voice thundered, then he made a step toward the door. "I'm starting to think the bastard is here and just laughing at us. What kind of person would do that?"

As he moved closer to the door, Carissa's fear escalated. "I—I was told he's been out of town on business."

He looked at her. "Who did you talk to—his secretary?"

Her defenses rose at his note of sarcasm. "She's also a good friend of mine."

"Really?" He frowned. "So, does this mean you *do* know C. J. Cartel?"

"No! I—I mean, I didn't know my good friend worked here until a few minutes ago. I only came here because you said that you were having trouble getting in to see Cartel, so I decided to see if I would have better luck." *I'm sinking fast.*

He stared at her for a moment. "So, did your friend tell you when her elusive employer will be back in town?"

"At least another two weeks."

"That long?" He exhaled and rubbed his hand along the short crop of his hair. "I don't know if I'll still be here then."

Her heart skipped a beat. "You're leaving?"

"I have some business to tie up in New York. I might be able to send my assistant. I don't know. My life's been a little crazy here lately."

"I can imagine. I've been experiencing a few hiccups myself."

"You want to tell me about it over dinner?"

"I don't think—"

"I missed you at the hospital today."

"I'm sorry." She gave up, running out of excuses. "I've really been busy."

"You've told me. Look, I get the hint and I understand. You won't get any more pressure from me. I'll make sure I keep my distance."

He moved away and a wave of panic washed over her. "Wait." Her courage fled when his dark gaze centered on her. "I've been awful toward you. I'm sorry." *Are you crazy? Let him go.*

"Go on," he agreed.

She laughed. "You purposely used this guilt tactic, didn't you?"

"I'm a desperate man."

"All right, you win."

"Really? Does that mean you agree to have dinner with me?"

"Dinner?"

"A lot's happened since the last time we've talked. You're a great listener."

"So now I'm your shrink?" Carissa crossed her arms, but a bright smile covered her face. "That means I should be charging you by the hour."

Nathan held up his hands in surrender. "Judging by that Armani suit, I don't think I can afford your prices. What did you say your family business was?"

"I didn't."

Again, he held up his hands. "Sorry. I didn't mean to pry. I suppose we all have our secrets. But I must say yours are stacking up pretty high."

"Have you ever thought that maybe you just ask too many questions? Just because you're Travis's son doesn't mean you're not some mass murderer."

He moved so close she feared he'd hear her heart pounding.

"Do you make a habit of kissing mass murderers?" His gaze caressed her face.

Speech failed her as her eyes lowered to his lips

and the memory of their kiss weakened her knees. And despite the afternoon's cool breeze, she felt hot.

"Now about that dinner. How about I pick you up at your place at eight o'clock?"

No. Say no. "Eight?"

"I'll tell you what. I'll even wear a tie."

She smiled at that. "Do you even own one?"

Nathan rubbed his chin in deep thought. "Good point. Are the malls still open?"

"That's okay." Carissa laughed. "I don't want you to go to any trouble. Dinner at eight will be fine." *That's if I don't hang myself by seven-thirty.*

Chapter 19

Nathan returned to his car rather pleased with himself. He smiled as he watched Carissa's SUV pull out of the parking deck. What was it about her that intrigued him so much? Maybe he was fascinated by how she went to such extremes to avoid him.

He started the car and laughed at his inflated ego. Instead of being pursued, he was doing the pursuing. It was a nice change. As he pulled out into traffic, his thoughts drifted to Carissa's other charming characteristics. But there was only one word that described Carissa: *mysterious*.

He couldn't fathom why she kept her hair pulled back or wore unflattering business suits. It was as if she went to great pains to hide herself.

He remembered their first meeting and how the morning sunlight seemed to dance off each curl of her hair. And her eyes, for the briefest moment, were so childlike. That was when he'd first felt stirrings of some kind.

But it was the kiss at her front door that monopolized his thoughts and even seeped into his dreams. He could tell a lot about a woman by her kiss. In Carissa's, he tasted passion and longing. It was that longing that haunted him.

"A date? A real date?" Helena shrieked.

Carissa cradled her head between her hands, feeling sick. "I was doing so well. Then I ran into the man twice in one day."

"Took one look into that man's handsome face and couldn't say no, huh?"

"Something like that. Oh, Auntie. Nothing good can come of this. It's like I have a death wish."

"Or you're just following your heart. Come on, stop your moaning and groaning." She glanced at her watch. "It's seven o'clock. I have less than an hour to perform a miracle."

"What are you talking about?" Carissa frowned when her aunt pulled her up from the sofa.

Helena stopped and dropped her hands on her hips. "You're not planning to go out dressed like that, are you?"

Carissa looked down at her attire. "Well, no."

"Do you have any idea what you're going to wear?"

"I haven't given it much thought."

"That's what I was afraid of." Helena shook her head, then grasped her niece's arm.

Minutes later, Carissa sat on her bed and stared incredulously at her aunt as she tossed outfits onto the bed. "What are you doing?"

"Praying." Helena turned and faced her. "Don't you own any evening wear?"

"They're in the other closet."

Her aunt clasped her hands together, then raced to the bedroom's second walk-in closet. Her face quickly fell in dismay. "This is your evening wear? There's nothing but business suits in here."

Carissa joined her. "No, they're not. They're casual pantsuits, not quite business suits. I find them perfect for banquets and business dinners."

Helena stared at her as if she'd sprouted another head. "This is worse than I thought. Come on." She snatched Carissa by the wrist and dragged her into the guest room, where she proceeded to go through her own wardrobe. "We need something simple, yet sexy."

Carissa picked up an outfit. Her eyes widened at the dress's plunging neckline.

"Oh, that will be perfect." Her aunt took the dress from her.

"For what—amateur night at the Gold Club?"

Helena shrugged. "You never know, he might like strippers."

Carissa crossed her arms and narrowed her gaze. "There's no way in hell I'm wearing that."

Helena glanced at her, then back at the outfit. "You're right. You don't have the chest for it."

"What? What's wrong with my chest?"

"Nothing. I'm just slightly more endowed. What about this one?" She held up a little black dress.

Carissa took the dress and inspected it. "Not bad. It's simple."

"And don't forget sexy," Helena added, twisting her hips.

"It's kind of short, don't you think?"

Helena reclaimed the dress. "It's supposed to be short. Trust me on this. When he takes one look at you tonight, he'll be putty in your hands."

Carissa smiled at the thought.

"Now that we have the outfit out of the way. Our next task is your hair. Do you have any scissors?"

She quickly pulled back. "You're crazy if you think I'm going to let you cut my hair."

"Relax. I'm just going to trim it up a little."

"Are you any better at cutting hair than you are at cooking?"

"You're comparing apples to oranges." Helena glanced at her watch. "You go ahead and jump in the shower. I'll get everything ready for your transformation. I can't wait until he sees you."

Nathan rang the doorbell at eight o'clock sharp. In his hand, he carried a single red rose. As he rocked back on his heels, he inhaled a deep breath. He couldn't remember ever being this nervous.

Helena answered the door, breathless. She took one look at him and her eyes brightened. "You don't happen to have another one of you at home, do you?"

He laughed at her candidness. "I'm sorry to disappoint you."

She stepped back and allowed him to enter.

Nathan stood in the entry and took in the penthouse's subtle elegance.

"It's not what you expected, huh?" Helena read his thoughts, then looked around, too. "You know, I was always taught that you can tell a lot by a person's home." She slid her arm around his and led him toward an exquisite portrait. "For instance, you can learn their passion."

He looked up at a beautiful ballerina that at first sight stole his breath. There was no mistaking the dancer's identity. "How old was she?"

"I believe eleven. Her father painted it."

"I didn't know he was an artist." He leaned closer "He had a wonderful eye."

"It's amazing what he captured, isn't it?" Helena crossed her arms and studied the picture with pride. "But he was what I called a closet artist. He never pursued it professionally. I remember teasing him about how he was depriving the world of his talent."

Nathan faced her. "I'm sorry for your loss."

Her smile wobbled. "Despite his flaws, and let me tell you he had plenty, he was a great brother."

"I'm sure he was."

"I'm sorry to keep you waiting," Carissa announced as she made her grand entrance.

Nathan looked up and simply stared at the creation before him. Her hair hung in perfect ringlets to her shoulders, while her face appeared luminous beneath the room's low lighting. His gaze traveled lower to her provocative black dress, and his mouth went dry.

Carissa's heart pounded in her ears as a wave of heat followed the wake of his gaze. There was no mistaking the gleam of approval in his eyes.

"You look amazing," he finally said with a widening smile.

Carissa shared a conspiratorial smile with her aunt.

"You two kids have a good time." Helena winked, then retreated to the guest room.

"I'm almost afraid to show you out on the town. Someone might steal you away." He walked toward her.

"Scared of a little competition?"

"Where you're concerned, yes."

She stood mesmerized as he drew near. "I brought this for you." He held out the rose.

"Red?"

He laughed. "I guess I wasn't thinking. Red is for lovers, isn't it?"

She managed to nod, but wondered how she remained standing.

"I promise next time I'll remember to bring yellow."

"Next time?"

"After seeing you in a dress like that, I'm anxious

to see what other little secrets you have hidden in your closets."

Unaccustomed to such flattery, she felt her face flush deep burgundy as she accepted his gift. "What makes you think I have secrets?"

"Don't all women?"

Chapter 20

If Carissa hadn't known any better, she would have sworn that she was a teenager on her way to her first prom. During the car ride, her stomach had twisted into knots, her palms were sweaty, and her knees knocked. But when she glanced at him, he appeared calm, cool and collected.

"Are you sure you don't mind going to this party? I promised a friend that I would put in an appearance."

"N-no. It'll give me a sneak peek into the life and times of Nathan Edwards." She teased him with a confident smile while her mind raced as to whether she'd bump into anyone she knew. "So what kind of crowd is this?"

He shrugged. "Well, the usual. Photographers, designers and models. And you know, where there are models there are—"

"Musicians," they said in unison, then laughed.

"Have you ever dated a model?" she asked.

"No. It's a rule of mine never to mix business with pleasure."

"Have you ever been tempted to break the rules?"

He laughed as if he'd been caught with his hand in the cookie jar. "Occasionally. How about you? You work in an office, I assume? Ever been attracted to someone you work with?"

"Never," she answered without hesitation.

"Well, what kind of man are you attracted to?"

"The kind in romance novels. Tall, dark and handsome." *Like you.*

Nathan's brows arched with interest. "Romance novels?"

She crossed her arms defensively. "You have a problem with that?"

"No, no. But why would you want to read about love instead of going out there and experiencing it? I mean, I can easily picture *you* draped across an Arabesque novel with some tall, dark and handsome man searching your face adoringly."

She laughed at his flair for dramatics as he struck ridiculous poses. "You just make sure you keep your eye on the road," she warned.

He straightened in his seat, then flashed her a sly smile. "You know, I've told you a lot about my past relationships. In fact, I've told you a lot about everything. Don't you think that tonight it's your turn to tell me a little more about yourself?"

Carissa's smile vanished and her earlier nervousness returned. "There's nothing to tell."

"Never been in love?"

She shrugged. "Don't make it sound like it's a crime. I made up my mind a long time ago to pursue a career. I've put everything I had into my job."

"Running your father's business?"

She nodded.

"What kind of business do you do?"

Damn. She closed her eyes. It was time for another lie. "Commercial real estate. Nothing half as exciting as what you do." *Now, let's hope he doesn't ask me anything about real estate.*

He nodded as if digesting the information. "You must be very good at it. You seem very successful. But it sounds lonely."

"No more than traveling the world three hundred days out of the year. Tell me, how much time did you spend with your ex?"

For the first time that night he didn't look so confident. "Are you trying to say that it's my fault she slept around?" He stared at her incredulously.

"Of course not." She took a deep breath. "I'm just saying that maybe we're responsible for our own loneliness."

Silence filled the car and Carissa wanted to kill herself for ruining the mood.

After Nathan parked, he turned to face her. "I

guess I can see your point." He nodded. "You know, there are no real accidents. Maybe all of this is happening for a reason."

Carissa stared at the glitzy club across the street and frowned at the overflowing crowd. She wasn't ready to give up the quiet intimacy of the car. "Before Edwards's…I mean, your father's attack, you never once entertained the idea of trying to make amends with him?"

He shook his head. "Too angry."

"And now?" She turned toward him, hoping to delay going into the club.

"Can't remember why or how I stayed that angry. I guess looking back on it, Smokey and I have always shared the same opinion of Travis's desertion. Maybe our anger fed off each other's."

"Smokey?" Carissa smiled to lighten the mood.

Nathan laughed. "He's my stepfather. Well, not really. He never actually married my mom. But I think they had considered themselves common law. Anyway, I've always thought of him as a father. From what I understand, back in the sixties—"

"You're not going to tell me that he's an ex-hippie, are you?"

"Ha-ha. No. He was a musician. The gigs he used to play were always in these smoke-filled clubs. After a while, his friends started teasing him about how the cigarette smoke would cling to his clothes. Then next thing he knew he was affectionately known as 'Smokey.'"

"It sounds like you two are very close."

"I like to think so. I mean, I don't get to see him often. We're both workaholics."

"Is he still a musician?"

"Nah. He's in the wonderful world of corporate America. Now, don't ask me what he does. It all sounds like pushing paper around to me."

When she laughed, he propped his arm up against the back of the seat and gazed at her. "Has anyone ever told you you have a beautiful laugh?"

"Thank you." Her throat constricted with emotion as she melted beneath his intense stare. How was it that he could make her feel so alive?

"I'm starting to hate that I promised to put in an appearance tonight. I'm not sure I want to share you with anyone else."

That makes two of us. "You still have a way of saying the right thing at the right time."

"I could say the same for you. If it hadn't been for you, I don't think I would have found the courage to let go of my anger and try to seek some type of closure in all of this. I guess what I'm trying to say is, you've inspired me to rise about the past. And I'm eternally grateful."

Carissa closed her eyes and wanted to cry. The whole situation had gotten out of control and she needed to do something fast. "Nathan, I think there's something I need to tell you."

Chapter 21

Carissa struggled for the right words while her eyes glossed over.

Nathan took her hand. "It's okay. If it's this hard for you to tell me, we can talk about it at another time, whenever you're ready."

"Okay." She nodded, still unable to speak.

"Come on. Let's go put in our appearance." He leaned over and kissed her cheek, then got out of the car.

He deserves much better than me, she thought as she watched him walk around to her door. He deserved someone honest and loving, not some callous CEO who wanted to play Cinderella.

He opened her car door and helped her out. His

gaze again assessed her figure. "You should have pursued modeling. You're perfect."

"If I had, we would be breaking your rule."

"It would have been worth it." He offered her his arm, then escorted her to the club.

When they stepped inside, a crowd of people gathered around them. Many just wanted to welcome Nathan to the party, others wanted to know where he'd been and what his next assignment would be.

Carissa was out of her element and soon felt invisible. Not to mention the music was three times too loud. Before she knew it, her heart seemed to pulse in time with the music's bass.

"Nate, there you are," a feminine voice exclaimed over the music. "I was beginning to think that you weren't coming."

Carissa watched as a beautiful woman approached them and embraced Nathan. And to her horror, he returned the affectionate gesture.

"You know that I'm a man of my word."

"I don't call you Honest Abe for nothing."

They laughed.

Carissa, uncomfortable by how striking they looked together, cleared her throat.

Nathan turned. "I'm sorry," he apologized. "Where are my manners? Aria, I'd like to introduce you to my date this evening, Carissa Carnes—affectionately known as Risa. Risa, I'd like for you to meet one of my *model* friends."

Carissa relaxed. *He never dates models,* she remembered before extending her hand. "It's nice to meet you."

The woman's cold hand slid into hers. "Likewise." Her smile missed her eyes. And Carissa sensed that the woman was looking down her nose at her.

"I didn't know you acquired a new playmate in Atlanta." Aria returned her attention to Nathan.

Carissa caught the insinuation that there were other women and was amazed that the thought had never occurred to her. Why not? He was incredibly handsome.

"Aria, behave," Nathan warned with a sharp look.

Aria smiled. "I'm always on my best behavior. You know that. But I was wondering how those nude shots turned out." Seduction gleamed in her eyes as she edged closer. "We never did finish what we started."

Carissa's face burned as her hands clenched at her sides. The audacity of this woman was outrageous.

"Would you care to dance?" a male voice questioned at Carissa's side before she had the chance to give Aria a piece of her mind.

She turned toward a handsome gentleman with an impressive athletic body.

"Actually, we were just about to leave," Nathan informed him.

"I'd love to." Carissa overruled him and accepted the man's hand. *Two can play this game,* she decided, heading toward the crowded dance floor.

Even though it had been years since she'd been in a club, she took one look around and quickly began imitating the dances of various couples surrounding her. Before she knew it, she was lost in the music and having the time of her life.

Nathan stood, fascinated, as Carissa and her partner became the center of attention. She was by far the best dancer on the floor. As he watched her, his gaze took in every inch of her. Why in the hell would a woman try to hide a body like that?

"I see you picked out a wild one," Aria whispered in his ear.

"Trust me, it's a news flash for me."

"Do you want to head on out there and stir up some of our own trouble?" She wrapped an arm around his waist.

Nathan exhaled, then turned to face her. "I'm quite happy with the date I brought. But thanks for asking."

"It looks to me that she's content with her partner on the dance floor."

"Only because of your trying to bait her into a catfight. Look, Aria, if you value me as a friend, please back off. I've told you before that I can only offer you friendship."

Her smile faltered. "Well, don't hold back. Tell me how you really feel." Sarcasm laced her voice, but then she quickly made an about-face. "But you're right. I do value our friendship and I'll back off. After all, a woman can only take so much rejection." She leaned over and kissed his cheek, then went off into the crowd.

Nathan smiled, pleased that he'd finally taken care

of that problem. He then turned his attention back to Carissa. However, after the fourth song, he wondered if she'd ever leave the dance floor.

When the next song started, her partner gave up trying to keep up with her, but another man was there to take his place. On the seventh song, Nathan cut into the number.

When she faced him, he couldn't mistake her look of irritation.

"Oh, you finally broke away from your Playboy centerfold?" she asked, never skipping a beat of the music.

"We parted company forty minutes ago," he informed her with a laugh.

"What's so funny?"

"I'm flattered by your jealousy."

She stopped. "I'm not jealous."

"Too bad." He shrugged as she continued to dance. "I know I was while you danced with every man here."

His confession caused a shiver of pleasure to race down her spine.

"Don't gloat," he warned, pulling her close. "And don't rob me of my dance."

She laughed, then continued grooving to the music.

Hours later, Carissa and Nathan decided to have dinner at Sambuca. During their meal, they were entertained by one of Atlanta's prominent jazz bands and served one of the best meals Carissa had ever tasted.

"Does your love for jazz come from your stepfather?" she asked him in between the band's sets.

"Among other things. He influenced my love for photography as well."

"Really?"

"Yep. He bought me my first camera when I was ten. I've never been able to put it down since."

"Sounds like you owe him a lot."

"I do." He glanced down at his half-eaten dinner. "I know my sudden concern for Travis has hurt him in some ways. I mean, I don't mean to make it sound as though he's jealous, but I can tell that he's hurt."

"Sounds a little selfish."

Nathan frowned. "I don't know if selfish is the right word."

"I'm sorry. That was uncalled-for. I don't know him."

"It's okay." He shrugged off her apology. "I think, in truth, he may feel threatened. It's understandable, I guess. In a way, I think he saved my mom and me when my father walked out. Times were rough and money was scarce. Had it not been for Smokey, I don't know what we would have done."

Carissa leaned her face against the palm of her hand as she listened.

"Of course, that's around the time he gave up his music career. He said that he wasn't making enough playing in small pubs, and I think he always harbored hopes that he and my mom would eventually have children. But it never happened."

"Were you all happy?"

"I thought so. For a while, anyway. Then my mother suffered with serious bouts of depression. Later, she started drinking. I don't think she ever got over my real father."

Carissa listened quietly as she sipped her drink.

"She died after washing down a handful of pills with a bottle of vodka. Smokey found her lying on the bathroom floor. The worst part for him was finding a love letter to Travis balled in her fist."

Carissa swallowed a lump in her throat. "So she loved him until the end?"

"Yeah." Nathan didn't meet her gaze. He continued to stare at his food.

"I think I understand why your stepfather feels so threatened." She reached for his hand.

"Do you still think I'm doing the right thing? Smokey has already lost my mother. I don't want him to think that he's going to lose me, too."

"Then you're going to have to assure him of that. But you also need to seek closure for yourself. Your stepfather has to understand that."

Nathan squeezed her hand. "I'm glad we met."

Carissa smiled. "I am, too."

Chapter 22

Nathan and Carissa once again stood outside her apartment door.

Her stomach fluttered in anticipation of a good-night kiss. Would it feel the same? Would she lie awake just thinking about it? God, she hoped so.

"Here we are," he announced, gazing down at her. "Are you as nervous as I am?"

"You're nervous?" she asked, astonished. "What do you have to be nervous about?"

"Are you kidding? The last time I kissed you, you avoided me for a week." He smiled down at her. "I don't want that to happen again."

"I don't think you have to worry about that. I really had a good time tonight."

"Does that mean you'll see me again?"

"Only if you shut up and kiss me."

Her gaze watched his lips as his head descended. And when they landed against hers, it was everything she'd hoped for and more. The gentle invasion of his tongue sent ripples of pleasure through her entire body. When their kiss deepened, her arms slid around his neck to pull him closer. She wanted to savor each moment.

Their lips parted, but her eyes remained closed as if she floated on an invisible cloud. Her knees weakened from the heat of his breath caressing her face. Nathan tilted her chin up with his finger.

"Can I see you tomorrow?"

She nodded, unsure if she'd be able to wait that long. "I'd like that."

"Good. I'll see you tomorrow." He kissed her again, then turned from the door.

As she did the last time, she watched him until he disappeared from sight. Only then did she exhale and enter her apartment.

"It's about time." Helena folded the magazine in her lap, then crossed her arms as she stared up at her. "I thought you'd never get home. Now, come on over here and tell the juicy stuff."

"What on earth are you doing up?" Carissa asked, grinning.

"Oh, you had a good time, didn't you? I can tell by that look on your face. Does that mean we get to keep him?"

"We?"

"You need a husband and I need some children running around here. I regret never having any and I'm trying to prevent you from making the same mistake. Life can seem awfully lonely without them."

Carissa joined her on the sofa. "I wish we could keep him, Auntie. But I don't know."

"You know, Risa. I've been trying to convince you to just come clean about what happened. I'm still sure he'll understand. But if you continue to put it off, then it will look like you intentionally deceived him. But if you want a relationship with him, then you're going to have to come clean—and soon." Helena stood. "We can talk about your evening over breakfast. Right now you need to think about what I said." She gathered her things and headed off to bed.

Later, Carissa lay in bed, staring up at the ceiling. For the most part, she tried to relive the evening in her mind. In the short time she'd known Nathan Edwards, her whole life had been turned upside down. She felt things she had never felt and dreamed things she had no right to dream.

If it all ended tomorrow, she would never regret the time she'd spent with him. But the question was whether she was prepared to lose it all.

No. She shook her head and sat up in bed. He could offer her more, she was sure of it. His eyes promised more. She thought of his strength, his sincerity, his honesty and even his vulnerability. She was attracted to all of his qualities. What would it be like to love and be·loved by such a man?

Carissa crossed her arms as if to hug herself. There was no way she deserved him, but that didn't stop her from wanting him. And there were times tonight, she was sure he wanted her, too. She smiled at the thought.

The phone's sudden shrill caused her to jump. "Hello."

"I can't sleep." Nathan's deep baritone drifted over the line. "What about you?"

She smiled against the phone. "I'm wide-awake."

"That's good news. I'd hate to have awakened you."

"I see you found my phone number."

"Yeah. It was thoughtful of you to slip it into my jacket tonight. It was a nice little surprise."

"Don't mention it. Thanks for calling."

"Are you kidding? I nearly broke my neck trying to get to the phone."

She continued to smile against the phone as they lapsed into a comfortable silence. "I really had a great time tonight," she finally said.

"Maybe I should come back over."

"So soon?"

"Why not? Don't you know what day it is?"

"What?"

"It's tomorrow already."

She laughed as she stretched back against the

pillows. They continued talking and laughing for hours. When the morning's first ray of sunlight streamed through her windows, Carissa slept curled in bed with the phone tucked beneath her ear.

Chapter 23

"I've finally found the woman of my dreams," Nathan declared, then whacked Smokey hard on the back. "Maybe I can bring her here to your place one night so you can meet her. I'm telling you, you're going to love her. She's intelligent, she's funny, and man, can she dance."

Smokey leaned back from his breakfast with an amused grin. "May I ask who the lucky girl is?"

"It's Carissa. Don't you remember I told you about her?"

"Oh, yeah. A Ms. Carnes, am I right?"

"That's the one."

"You found out that she was available and didn't waste any time."

Nathan took the last bite of his pancakes, then washed it down with his coffee before he responded. "I didn't mean for anything to happen."

Smokey arched his brows questioningly.

"Okay, maybe on some level I was always attracted to her. But I'm telling you, when you meet her you'll understand where I'm coming from. Then again, I know at times she can come off as a bit uptight."

"I remember you saying that last week."

"But I'm telling you, Pop, she knows how to let her hair down. You should have seen her dancing at the party last night. She had every man there wanting her."

"You being no exception."

Nathan waved off his sarcasm. "I can't explain it."

"Well, she really must be something to get you talking a hundred miles an hour. But don't you think you're rushing things? I mean, come on, you just met the girl."

"That's another thing," Nathan added. "It doesn't *feel* like we just met. Not for me anyway. I've been so comfortable talking to her about personal issues almost from the beginning. And she listens—truly listens to what I have to say."

Smokey slapped his hand on the table with a wide grin. "Then that settles it. You better marry her. It's hard to find a listener out there. I tell you what—I'm going to start hanging out at the hospital, too. I didn't know it was such a hot spot to find women."

Nathan laughed. "You think I'm crazy, don't you?"

"It doesn't matter what I think. But whatever happened to being cautious? You wouldn't want to repeat the whole India fiasco."

"Caution be damned." Nathan laughed. "Believe it or not I'm ready to jump into this relationship with blinders on."

"I don't know, son. It sounds risky."

"Yeah, that it is. But I got to tell ya, it feels great."

Helena listened as Carissa sang in the shower, whistled while she cleaned up, and hummed as she worked on her laptop.

"My God, girl. You've got it bad." Helena propped her hands on her hips.

"Got what bad?" Carissa asked, looking up from her work.

"The love bug. And stop trying to act like you don't know what I'm talking about. There's more music coming out of you than the Atlanta Symphony Orchestra."

"Very funny."

Helena leaned against her work table. "It may be funny, but it's also true. That man must have rocked your world."

"I told you last night, we had a good time."

"Are you going to see him again?"

"We're going to a movie tonight."

"A drive-in, I hope."

Carissa's smile widened. "As a matter of fact, we are."

"Oh, so you did inherit some of my genes. There may be hope for you yet, sweetheart. But what are you going to do about that other little issue we talked about?"

"I'm going to tell him the truth."

"That's great," Helena exclaimed, reaching over to hug her. "I bet you he's going to understand everything."

Carissa shut off her computer and stood up. "Well, I hope you're right. I don't know what I'll do if he ends up hating me." She headed toward the door. "I'm going over to see Liz. I want to make sure she's doing all right. I trust you can entertain yourself until I get back."

"Not a problem. I need to do something about rounding up a man, too. I'll be damned if you're the only one with a date on a Saturday night."

Liz opened her front door and blinked in surprise at seeing her boss. Then her gaze swept over her free-flowing hair and her flawless makeup. And was she wearing jeans?

"Ms. Cartel—what are you doing here?"

"I came to see how you were doing."

Confused, Liz stared.

"I would have been here sooner, but I got lost trying to find your street. I must have passed by here six or seven times," she added with an awkward smile. "May I come in?"

Liz broke from her trance and jumped back. "Of

course. Forgive me. Things are a little hectic right now."

"Please, there's no need to apologize."

The women stood, smiling awkwardly at one another, before Liz broke the silence. "I just can't believe you're here."

"I wanted to come." Carissa remembered the box in her hands. "Oh, this is for you. I thought it would be a nice change from you always buying me things."

"You shouldn't have."

"I wanted to."

"Won't you come into the living room and sit down?"

"I'd love to." Carissa admired the modest home as she followed her. "You know, Liz, I never knew you drove so far to work every day. What is it—thirty miles?"

"Yeah, it's quite a stretch. Can I get you something to drink?"

"No, thanks. I just polished off a bottle of water in the car."

"Okay." Liz sat down, then opened her package. She gasped in surprise as she pulled out the old black and white photo of Liz's grandparents that had sat on her desk. Now it was in the most exquisite silver frame she'd ever seen.

"I hope you like it."

"It's beautiful," she said in awe.

"I really didn't know what to get you, which is a shame, really. You've worked every day outside my office for the past eight years and I never took the time to try to get to know you."

"It's okay, Ms. Cartel. I hope you forgive me for what I said to you yesterday. I had no right to say those things."

"Actually, I'm glad you did. There was a lot of truth to what you said." Carissa looked down at her hands. "You remember the snowball you bought me for my birthday?"

"Of the little ballerina?"

"Yeah. It was a beautiful gift. But I have to admit, at first I was saddened by it, because it reminded me of who I wanted to be when I was younger. I think, subconsciously, I've never forgiven myself for giving up on my dreams." She looked up at Liz's warm smile.

"I'm glad you shared that with me. It means a lot."

Carissa wiped at her eyes. "Now back to you. I'm here to help you. What can I do?"

"Actually, everything is pretty much taken care of. I've been preparing for this day for a long time. As soon as Darius wakes from his nap we're going to a cousin's house for preparations for the wake."

"How did he take the news?"

"He handled it well. I must say he did better than I did. Actually, he's been full of surprises here lately. You know when Mr. Edwards's son first came to the office last week, Darius took to the man like a fish to water."

"Really?"

"I've never seen anything like it. He's always been so shy around strangers."

"So he has a way with children?"

"I'd say. I was just about ready to send Darius to a child psychiatrist. Nathan Edwards gave me hope that this is just a phase."

Carissa liked the thought of Nathan surrounded by children.

"Ms. Cartel, are you all right?"

"Oh, I'm fine." She waved off her concern. "I was just daydreaming."

"It must have been some dream to put a smile like that on your face."

"Trust me, it was. But, Liz, if we're going to be friends, please stop calling me Ms. Cartel when we're not working. Call me Carissa—or Risa, whichever you prefer."

"You got a deal, Risa."

Carissa managed to locate the private room Travis had been transferred to with little difficulty. She'd wanted to see him for a while and was grateful that she'd picked a time when Nathan was away.

The moment she saw Travis propped up against the pillow, she worried that he looked so pale. She moved toward the bed and reached for his hand. *It's still cold.*

"Please help him through this," she prayed through building tears. She pulled a chair over to the bed and sat down. For a long time, she just held his hand and struggled for the right words to say.

"I feel strange about coming here again," she began. "But I had to. I don't want to make the same mistake twice." She closed her eyes and laughed at herself. "You have no idea of what I'm talking about. You see, years ago I refused to come see my father when he was lying in the hospital. Mainly, because I was scared. I figured if I didn't say goodbye, then he wouldn't leave. Silly, huh?"

The heart monitors beeped in response and another sad laugh erupted from her. "I swear I didn't mean to hurt him. But I did. I know I did because I did it so many times before. I look back now and remember what happened the night of his heart attack. We were fighting…again. He was angry with me for sneaking out of the house so I could be with my friends— friends that I don't even have anymore.

"He claimed that I was a disgrace and that I'd never amount to anything. Basically, it was the same argument that we always had." She fell silent as her emotions overwhelmed her.

When she finally looked up again, it wasn't Travis she saw lying in the bed, nor was it his hand she held—it was her father's. "I'm sorry, Daddy. I'm so sorry for everything I did to hurt you. Will you ever forgive me?" Carissa released his hand and covered her face as tears fell freely from her eyes.

A strong hand settled on her shoulder and she jumped up from her chair. But when she saw Nathan standing there with outstretched arms, she rushed into his embrace and cried until her river of tears had dried.

Chapter 24

For the next two weeks, Nathan and Carissa spent every evening together, whether it was enjoying a movie or talking well into the morning at the hospital's cafeteria. However, at the beginning of each date, Carissa had every intention of telling Nathan the truth, and each time she chickened out. Just as she had again tonight.

"I want to take a picture of you."

"Excuse me?" Carissa jerked her gaze up and drowned in the dark pools of his eyes. Their intensity was so direct, she felt vulnerable beneath them.

Nathan's hand traced her jawline and something blissfully erotic stirred at her core.

"I bet a face like yours could make love to the

camera for hours." His voice lowered to a husky timbre.

It took everything she had to remain standing and not to swoon in the man's arms like a lovesick teenager. Everything about him played havoc with her senses and preoccupied her mind with visions of making love to him in some interesting position.

She licked her parched lips and witnessed how his gaze followed the movement as if in a trance. For one brief moment, she was aware of her own power, and she reveled in it.

"Are you interested?"

"In what?" She blinked, confused by the question.

"Posing for me. I don't think that I'll ever forgive myself if I don't get you in front of the camera. I'd do you in black and white with very little lighting, but with enough to catch that subtle glimmer in your eyes."

Carissa wasn't sure whether she was breathing as she hung on his every word and basked in the scent of his cologne.

"I'm fascinated by that spark. It's as if it holds a secret."

"What kind of secret?" She couldn't help but ask.

"You tell me."

She straightened. The insinuation struck too close to home. Her guilt tried again to convince her to come clean, but his earlier speech about honesty trapped her confession in her throat.

Nathan covered her hand and her gaze returned to his.

"Do you want to know what I think the secret is?"

She couldn't bring herself to answer.

"I think there's more to you than what meets the eye. I don't think the real you is this well-polished, overly independent woman you try to portray."

"Oh, really?" Carissa bit back her laughter. "I think you're definitely barking up the wrong tree on that one."

He gave her that familiar sly grin, the one she was beginning to love. "I don't think so." He reached up and tucked a lock of hair behind her ear. "I love your hair down."

She heard a snap and realized he'd opened the hair clip at the nape of her neck. Her hair tumbled free and she was shocked at how exposed she felt.

"You have beautiful hair," he whispered as he leaned closer.

His warm breath caressed her cheek and she had the distinct feeling that he was going to kiss her, and she was helpless to do anything about it. It would be so easy to submit to him. The notion eased into her thoughts and excited every fiber of her being. She wanted him.

Nathan needed her, more than he needed the air he breathed. He couldn't remember ever needing anything or anyone this much. At this moment, he could neither remember anything about life before her nor imagine life without her. His hand settled on the back of her head, and gently, he pulled her forward, hoping against hope that she wouldn't resist.

She didn't.

The moment their lips met, a jolt of electricity surged throughout his body, and he pressed her closer. Her firm breasts crushed against his chest and his control shattered.

Drunk with desire, his mouth ravished hers as he sought to satisfy a hunger he couldn't name or control. Her wine-flavored lips were sweet, yet intoxicating with an unbridled passion. Her nails dug into his back, wrenching a guttural moan from deep within his soul. He'd never known a pain he'd loved half as much.

No matter how hard he tried, he couldn't get close enough. It wasn't enough to simply be with her. Her arms promised something more.

Their lips tore apart. The sudden rush of air burned his lungs. It was then he tasted her salty tears.

"Did I hurt you?" He was surprised at the deep rasp of his voice and even the higher note of tenderness it held.

She shook her head. "I don't believe that you can ever hurt me." She wiped at her tears, then nestled her head between his shoulder and neck.

He held her, not knowing what to say or do. However, one thing remained clear—he wanted to make love to her.

Carissa tried to calm the frantic beating of her heart, wondering where she'd lost control, and how on earth she was going to reclaim it. Those thoughts didn't last long. She was distracted by his heart's irregular heartbeats. Was he feeling what she was at that moment?

God, she hoped so.

"Stay with me tonight."

The proposal sucked the wind out of her and the room became excruciatingly quiet. Slowly, she pushed back from his chest, sure that her surprise somehow mirrored in her eyes.

"I dare you to say yes."

Her brows arched and a smile brightened her face. "You know how I feel about dares."

"That's what I'm banking on."

She shook her head. "You're impossible."

"True, but the challenge still stands." Nathan leaned down and his lips brushed teasingly across hers, and she knew that there was no way she was going to turn down this challenge.

"We are just talking about pictures, right?"

"There is that."

She smiled wickedly. "And what else?"

His broad grin sobered as he tilted up her chin. "Why don't we wing this one? There're no rules or guidelines—let's just be impetuous together."

A shiver of excitement slithered down her spine. She had never been presented with a better offer.

"So what do you say?" he asked with a knowing smile.

"Show me that camera." She accepted his challenge and immediately loved the liquid rush of excitement coursing throughout her body. She turned from his stunned yet covetous eyes and sauntered back toward his self-made studio. His sure footing came quickly behind her.

Once in the room, Carissa's heart skipped a beat, but she was more than determined to rise to the challenge of this dare. She inhaled a deep cleansing breath, then forced her trembling fingers to work the tiny buttons of her blouse.

"Hold on a sec."

His voice jumped out at her, causing another moment of hesitation to fester. Nathan scrambled to the surrounding lighting equipment that at first blinded her but then were covered with thin films of red and blue filters. The ambience created by the drastic lighting armed her with the confidence she needed. She transformed into an actress preparing for the role of a lifetime.

He flipped a switch and jazz filtered into the room from speakers somewhere above her. When he reached for a camera, she saw him in his natural element—and it turned her on.

"I'm ready when you are."

His husky voice slid over her like a thin caress, and her fingers resumed unbuttoning. Her breath entered and escaped in thin wisps, but her body had already begun to sway gently to the music.

Nathan thought he'd died and gone to heaven. He had never waited with such eager anticipation to peek at a model before—or to peek at any woman.

The last button undone, Carissa peeled back her

blouse and revealed a beautiful, royal-blue bra. The delicate lacing accentuated her ample breasts and confirmed what he suspected all along: she was a woman with many secrets. Almost as an afterthought, he snapped the picture.

Carissa smiled. But it was different from the ones he had seen before; it held an unusual cockiness—as if she knew she had his undivided attention and that *she* was in complete control of everything.

She was right.

A wayward curl tumbled in front of her face, and the urge to run his fingers through her thick mane quickened his pulse. His chest muscles tightened at the sight of the slow decline of her hand. It pulled at the button tucked at the side of her hip, then unzipped the figure-hugging material. The skirt pooled at her feet.

Nathan grew hard. He stared at a pair of curvaceous legs arched on narrow pumps that seemed to go on forever. He doubted that he'd ever seen such perfection.

Her matching panties, with their low V-cut, drew and held his attention. He took another snapshot. She turned and stepped out from the circle of clothes, then kicked them out of view, but most important displayed the narrow string of her thong.

The camera clicked.

The next track on the stereo picked up the tempo and her body accommodated its rhythm.

Nathan's brows stretched in surprise. "I see I have a dancer on my hands," he teased, moving closer.

"Among other things." She shimmied her shoulders and winked provocatively at him.

The pictures snapped in rapid succession as both parties enjoyed their game.

For Carissa, her exhilaration became addictive. She loved the feelings she was experiencing and didn't want to think about stopping. She gave him her back, her body still gyrating in sync with the music.

She dared herself to go further.

Pinching the delicate material between her breasts, she unhooked her bra, then performed a dramatic turn as she peeled the undergarment from her body.

Nathan stopped.

Carissa soared.

At that moment in time, she was everything he wanted and she knew it. She moved toward him with the grace of a cat, then knelt down to meet his gaze. "I think it's my turn to operate the camera," she said.

The comment won a few notes of laughter. "I don't think so."

"Chicken?" she baited.

"No. You're just a hard act to follow."

She took the camera. "Dancing isn't a requirement."

Nathan's eyes lowered and once again became fascinated by her body. "You're so beautiful." He inhaled the soft floral fragrance of her hair and felt a primal yearning take root.

She tilted her head up; her breasts brushed against him and sent a surge of heat through him. Carissa snapped his picture, then slowly crawled backward with a command. "Follow me."

As Carissa slithered backward, Nathan crawled forward much like a game of cat and mouse.

"I don't think you know what you're getting yourself into." His eyes glittered as a warning.

"I'm willing to take my chances," she baited back with a wink. "That's if you're game."

"Careful. I just might have to see how far you're willing to go."

Carissa stopped in the center of the tarp and pulled up onto her knees while fumbling with the camera.

"You don't even know how to work that thing." His face lit with amusement.

The camera clicked and she rewarded him with a look of triumph. "Strike a pose," she directed.

Nathan willed his grinning features to sober while he tried to transmit his energy, hunger and desire through his eyes. He wanted her to feel how much he wanted her.

Maxwell's smooth, angelic voice floated from the surrounding speakers and Carissa's light bantering ceased. The room tilted and she couldn't seem to moisten her lips or control her erratic heartbeat.

He continued to edge closer, forcing Carissa to bend backward until she adjusted her body to lie flat on her back while he hovered above her. "Now, this is more like it," he said, taking the camera from her hands.

Speech eluded Carissa as he vision blurred. Yet she

saw Nathan with startling clarity. She reached beneath his turtleneck and glided her hands along hard, corded muscles.

"Do you know how long I've waited for this?"

His whispered words caressed the shell of her ear and her eyes drifted closed as she shook her head in response.

"All my life," he admitted truthfully. If there were such a thing as a soul mate, it was the woman in front of him. "I want to make love to you."

Carissa's heart performed a somersault as any reasoning she had left vanished. Her eyes lowered to his mouth and her body quaked in anticipation.

"Do you want me?"

The question caught her off guard and forced her eyes to meet his steady gaze. She nodded.

"Let me hear you say it."

Her heart squeezed. "I want you."

His lips curved triumphantly as his body lowered to cover hers.

At the feel of his hard arousal pressed wantonly against the thin material of her panties, Carissa arched insistently against him as her soft moans blended with the beguiling music embracing them.

Beauty, peace and freedom gripped her, and she rode their repetitive waves with abandon, exhilarated by her newfound freedom. She wanted and needed him and she made sure that she spent the rest of the night showing him just how much.

Chapter 25

Somewhere between midnight and dawn, a lazy smile of satisfaction eased across Carissa's face. It was the best she'd felt in years. She inhaled Nathan's masculine scent and her body tingled in response. She moaned and edged closer.

"Whatcha thinking about?" Nathan's warm and inviting voice drifted in the dark.

Her eyes fluttered open. "You're awake?"

"I'm not sure. Seeing you lying next to me must mean I'm still dreaming."

She emitted a low laugh. "There you go saying the right things at the right time."

"Is that right?"

His smile gleamed in the moonlight and stole her

breath. While her vision adjusted to the dim lighting, she allowed herself the luxury of etching more details of his features into her memory.

His head lowered until their foreheads met. "I can come up with a few things you do right at the right time, too."

The darkness hid her blush. "You're impossible." She punched playfully at his chest.

"Maybe. But you're changing the subject—as usual."

His heavy arms appeared suddenly and pulled her forward. She melted beneath the warm caress of his breath and she found herself wishing that this night would never end.

"Now, tell me what you were thinking about earlier."

"That's easy. The same thing I'm thinking about now—you."

His body stiffened and the slight movement pleased her.

Idly, he twirled a lock of her hair around his finger. "What took you so long to come into my life, Risa?"

His serious tone sobered her flirtatious thoughts and even brought tears to her eyes. "I could ask you the same thing."

"Ah, but I think I have an answer." He shifted slightly and pressed a feathery kiss against her lips. "I think for a long time, I was afraid of you—or rather the thought of you."

"Why would you be afraid of me?"

"You represent so much—commitment, loyalty, everything that would cause any sane man to break out into a cold sweat."

Her brows heightened. "Don't be so cocky. That list scares the hell out of me, too."

"Oh, really?" He laughed. "I guess I had you pegged wrong."

"It wouldn't be the first time."

"A point well-made. I had you figured out to be a woman who's committed to having the best in life— to being the best in whatever you choose to do. I see so much fire and determination in your eyes that I have no doubts that you're loyal and you expect loyalty from those around you."

At her long silence, he asked, "How am I doing?"

She peeked beneath the sheets. "I'm half expecting you to pull out a crystal ball."

He guided her hands away as he laughed. "Tell me your secrets."

Her smile faltered. "A real woman never tells."

"And you're definitely that. But surely you can tell me something. This is developing into a one-sided relationship."

"That's not true. I've told you plenty of things I've never told anyone."

"Yeah, yeah. But I want to hear about the juicy stuff. Ex-boyfriends, one-night stands, or three-somes—"

"What?"

"Come on, don't act coy." His firm body pressed against her. "I know you have some dirty little secrets locked in a closet somewhere."

"You're right on both counts."

Nathan tickled her sides. "Come on, tell me."

Carissa screamed with laughter and tried desperately to pull away, but his hovering body jailed her.

"Okay, okay. I'll talk," she shouted. Tears trailed from her eyes.

"You promise?"

"Yes!"

He stopped. "Now tell me a secret."

"This has been blown out of proportion," she said, wiping her eyes. "I don't know what you want me to say."

"How about telling me something that turns you on. Can you handle that?"

She closed her eyes and shook her head. "I can't believe we're doing this."

"Hey, you promised." His hands descended.

"All right, all right. If you must know, I have this thing about blindfolds."

"Oh, really?" He rolled onto his side, still facing her.

Despite the room's darkness, Carissa sensed that he could see her embarrassment clearly. "How about you?" She tried to ease out of the spotlight.

"You know me. I'm your typical voyeur."

She laughed. "I knew you would say that."

"What else?"

"What do you mean 'what else'? That's enough, don't you think?"

"We can steer clear of turn-ons if you want to, though I don't know why. It was just starting to get good. We definitely have to try that blindfold thing."

"You won't get any objections from me," she teased, loving their jovial foreplay.

Nathan's voice once again penetrated her thoughts. "You claim to have been such a rebel as a teenager. Were there any hot, forbidden romances that had your father threatening to lock you in your room and throw away the key?"

"Are you kidding? He threatened to do that daily." She laughed at the memory. "There is something I haven't told you. I was engaged once."

"I thought you said that you've never been in love before."

"I haven't. Hence, I broke it off."

Nathan propped on his elbows and stared down at the outline of her face. "You're not about to tell me that you really were engaged to my father, are you?"

"Not likely." She laughed at the absurd thought.

His head dropped back onto the pillow. "You scared me there for a moment. I'd hate to think that someone won your heart before me," he added.

"You're awfully sure of yourself."

Gently, his finger traced the lining of her lips. "I'm sure about a lot of things lately."

So am I.

"Now finish telling me about this fiancée."

Hell, she could barely remember to think, much less talk. "Let's see. I think it went something like— I hit thirty, thought that I heard my biological clock banging in my ears, so I panicked and proposed to the first man that was brave enough to ask me out more than once."

"*You* proposed to him?"

"I know, I know. But you don't see me in my other life. I see what I want and I go after it." She didn't mean for her voice to sharpen, but it had and she turned her face in embarrassment.

"Said in that light, it doesn't sound like you're a very nice person in this other life of yours."

She shook her head, amazed at the web of deception she'd tangled herself in.

"You're real good at this pillow talk," he complimented.

"Is that what this is?"

"It's either that or foreplay."

"I like the sound of both of those," she teased, then placed a quick kiss against his lips. "A girl could definitely get used to this kind of thing."

"Does that mean we have another date for tomorrow night?"

"Only if you play your cards right."

"Is that right? Come here, you big tease."

When his mouth covered hers, she gave into the blissful pleasure of his lips and enjoyed more than their erotic taste, their passionate promises, or lustful yearnings—she simply enjoyed being with him.

* * *

Later that morning, sunlight crept through the clouds and illuminated the exhausted couple. Nathan lay propped on his side enjoying the ethereal beauty lying at his side. The intensity of last night haunted and excited him. He'd never experienced such passion. He wondered at its source and whether it would always be this way with her.

He brushed his fingers along the side of her face, trying to envision just that. He could get used to this, he thought. There were a lot of things he could get used to involving Carissa Carnes.

Carissa stretched languorously in the early morning sunlight with a spreading grin and a tranquillity she'd never known. Bits and pieces of last night's episode filtered into her thoughts. She laughed at her boldness and edged closer to him.

"Good morning."

Her eyes fluttered open. "Is it?" She smiled.

"Well, if I had to judge, I'd say this is the best morning I've ever had." He peered deep into her eyes as he shifted closer. "What about you?"

"I'd have to review my mental Rolodex, but I feel confident in agreeing with you." She wiggled her brows, still feeling flirtatious.

He pulled her beneath him and covered her mouth with a kiss.

Her arms encircled him, pulling him closer as her world spun blissfully out of control. When he drew back, she blinked several times before focusing.

"I'm in the mood for breakfast in bed." His husky whisper drifted across her ear.

She moaned. "That means that one of us will have to get out of bed."

He shook his head. "I'm not referring to food." He lowered to take in an erect nipple and savored her instant gasp of pleasure.

Carissa's body came alive at the intimate touch of his hands and behaved in such ways that she no longer recognized it as her own. But how wickedly erotic it all felt.

At noon, they were finally hungry enough to get out of bed. Nathan slid into a pair of black and white pajama pants, while she draped on the matching top. Minutes later, she sat perched on a barstool, clapping while he showed her his way of making flapjacks.

Everything was perfect—he was perfect.

"How would you like your eggs, Ms. Carnes?"

Her smile froze as she lowered her hands to the counter. Whenever he called her by her fake last name, it was like a splash of cold water.

"Are you all right?" he asked. His concern instantly marred his features.

She waved absently in the air. "Oh, nothing. I was just thinking about something—it's nothing important."

"You sure?" His gaze lingered on her.

"Positive. Scrambled, if you don't mind."

When he returned his attention to cooking, Carissa's guilty conscience took over. *How can you say you love this man when he doesn't even know your name?* She closed her eyes against the war raging within her. And she knew for the first time she had to come clean—and soon.

She shook her head as she stood and walked away, then feigned interest in the apartment's decor. "You have an eye for art," she complimented absently.

"And an eye for beautiful women."

She rewarded him with a smile. "This one is a hungry woman."

"I got the hint. Give me a few more minutes."

She nodded, then returned her attention to assessing the apartment. Her gaze instantly swept across a nearby bookcase, then swung back when a familiar face leaped out at her. She moved closer. "Well, I'll be damned."

"Breakfast is served," Nathan announced proudly.

Carissa jumped.

He frowned. "What is it?"

Opening her mouth to dispel the notion that anything was wrong, she thought better of it and decided to have her curiosity sated. "This picture," she said, pointing. "Who's this man you're posing with in the picture?"

Nathan's gaze went to the silver-framed picture before a broad smile covered his face. "Ah, that would be the most important man in my life. My stepfather, Smokey."

Carissa's heart sank as she turned back to stare openly at the image of her vice president, Colin Hunter.

Chapter 26

Carissa angrily paced the floor of her office as her mind reeled with this latest twist. *What in the hell is going on?* Hunter had been the mastermind behind acquiring Edwards Electronics. Had he used her for—for what? *Revenge* was the only word that came to mind. But revenge for what?

She jabbed the intercom button on the phone. "Is Hunter in yet?"

"No, ma'am." The temp secretary, Maria, stammered over the line.

Clamping her jaw, Carissa punched the release button and returned to pacing. What the hell was Hunter's angle? What was the real reason he pushed to acquire Edwards Electronics? The more she thought about it, the more she felt certain that she'd been used.

The feeling didn't sit well with her.

The speaker beeped before Maria's accented voice filled the room. "Ms. Cartel, Mr. Hunter is here to see you."

"Show him in." She spun toward the desk, her hands clenched. "Calm down," she recited under her breath.

The door opened and Colin entered the room.

Carissa waited patiently until he closed the door behind him. "You have an awful lot of explaining to do."

"Is that so, Ms. *Carnes?*"

Her chin jerked as if he'd struck her.

"Don't act so surprised," he said coolly and with more reserve than she cared for. "I had to admit when my son first told me about you, I suspected, but I didn't quite put two and two together. But I figured it out. Though I have to admit I don't understand your angle."

"There's no angle. When I first met Nathan I just thought if he learned that I was Cartel that he would blame me for Travis's condition."

"And as time went on, you never felt the need to tell him the truth?"

"Under the circumstances, I hardly think that you're one to preach about honesty. What's your game in all of this?"

"You know how you always seem to think that

nothing is personal. Well, my dear, I'm here to tell you that everything is personal. Everything!"

"So I'm right. You did stage this!"

"Of course not. I had no idea of Travis's medical problems. I merely wanted to put the man out of business."

"But how convenient that it worked out this way for you," she added sarcastically.

He shook his head. "You have it all wrong."

"Do I?" She moved toward him. "You personally proposed that Cartel Enterprises acquire Edwards Electronics."

"True," he agreed, then shook his finger in the air. "But don't try to make this into anything more than it is. It was a golden opportunity that fell into our laps."

"No!" She closed the distance between them and jabbed a finger in the center of his chest. "This was a golden opportunity for you. You used my company to get what you wanted. I don't know for what—but revenge is written all over this fiasco."

"And since when did you object to that? Hell, since when did anyone in your family object? Do you even know the history of this company?"

The truth delivered a powerful blow and a curtain of shame covered her. She returned to her desk and leaned back in her chair. "Do I at least get to hear the real story between you and Edwards?"

The corners of her lips curved, but then he shrugged as his voice dripped with sarcasm and his hard gaze met hers. "Have you ever been in love with someone who loved another?"

Taken aback by the sudden flash of vulnerability in his eyes, she shifted uncomfortably in the chair.

"It's a living hell," he went on. "The worst part is I still love her. I loved her the moment I laid eyes on her."

"What stopped her from loving you?"

"She was married to my best friend."

"So I was right. This *was* all about revenge." It was a statement, not a question, and she was saddened by the reality of it. "But she loved Travis to the end, didn't she?"

He didn't respond.

"This is all going to blow up when Nathan learns the truth."

Colin's face sobered. "You mean this is going to blow up in *your* face, Miss Carnes." He sat in the vacant chair in front of her desk.

He was right. She was the only one. She was the only one who stood to lose everything. Her eyes narrowed with suspicion. "He can't possibly know you work here. Hell, Liz and I were a two-woman circus trying to prevent him from learning my real identity. If he knew about you, he would have simply come to you."

When he squirmed slightly in his chair, she knew she had him.

"Hasn't anyone ever told you that silence can also be viewed as dishonesty? There's no way he's not going to think that we somehow collaborated to do his father in."

Colin's face colored. "I will *not* lose my son."

"You mean stepson, don't you?"

"I've been that boy's father for most of his life. As far as I'm concerned all of this is your fault."

"What? How in the hell do you figure that?"

"Nathan would have left Atlanta a long time ago if it hadn't been for you. My son wouldn't have cared one bit if Travis Edwards dropped dead. Then you came along preaching love and forgiveness, which was the last thing I expected from C. J. Cartel."

The insult sparked her temper. "You have a lot of nerve, Hunter. If cold and ruthless is what you had in mind, maybe I should go and have a long talk with Nathan. Let him be the judge of whether you're guilty or not. We both know how he feels about honesty."

"He would never turn his back on me. I'm family."

"But you're not blood."

Colin jumped to his feet. "What the hell do you know?"

"I know that the one power Travis has is he's Nathan's flesh and blood. That's the real reason *your* son is still here. It didn't take much from me to convince him to let go of his anger. Anger that you no doubt fueled."

Carissa steepled her hands against her chin. "How on earth do you think you're innocent in any of this? You stole your best friend's wife, raised his child, then decided to swing the final ax by stealing his company." She shook her head again. "Remind me never to get on your bad side."

"That wasn't exactly how it was."

"But it's exactly how it turned out. And no matter how innocent you want to make yourself, when Edwards comes out of his coma, Nathan is going to be right there and you're *not* going to come out smelling like a rose and you know it."

His stony facade cracked.

"Think about it. For the first time, Travis has his son's undivided attention. Trust me, when he wakes up, we're screwed."

Nathan felt as if he were walking on a cloud as he strode down the hallway toward his father's room. He couldn't remember ever feeling this way. For the first time in his life he had hope for the future. He had someone in his life he looked forward to seeing and talking to every day. Not to mention he had someone he trusted.

Carissa made him feel like he could talk to her about anything. And to his amazement, he discovered that he wanted to tell her everything about his life.

Unfortunately, he realized, there was still a lot he didn't know about her. His pace slowed. Actually, there was quite a bit missing. He shrugged off the nagging feeling.

Of course, he knew plenty about her, except what she did for a living. He thought of last night's performance. She definitely could have a future as a stripper.

Nathan entered his father's private room. When he glanced at his father, to his surprise, he noticed there was more color in his complexion. Nathan's smile widened with hope. He sat next to the bed for a few seconds and allowed the monitors to be the only sound in the room.

Finally, he took Travis's hand into his. "I don't know about you, but when you're finally able to walk out of here, I plan to make up for lost time. It may be a little difficult, seeing that I do travel quite a bit." His thoughts returned to Carissa. "But I have a feeling that I'm going to be spending a lot of time in Atlanta." He laughed.

"You know I've been trying to remember the sound of your voice, but for the life of me I can't." He fell silent as his mind drifted.

"I remember for a long time, when you were away in Vietnam, I'd wait for hours by the door for you. Mainly because Mom kept saying that you were coming home soon, but it felt like a lifetime. But then you were gone again." He lowered Travis's hand and stood.

"Mom cried for a long time." As he moved toward the window he had a harder time shrugging off years of heartache and disappointment. "But the one thing I picked up on was the fact that she never said, 'Daddy will be home soon.' It's kind of funny what a child remembers, isn't it?"

Nathan exhaled. "Carissa said I'd feel better once I talked to you about this. It looks like she was right." He turned and choked back his shock when he stared down into Travis's eyes.

Chapter 27

Carissa drove for hours, terrified by the different scenarios of Nathan's possible reaction to her upcoming confession. And in her mind's eye, there was no way to escape the explosion—or rejection.

She shook her head at how everything had gotten so complicated. But the how and the why didn't matter anymore. She needed to focus on fixing it—no matter how much she dreaded it.

Even still, a glimmer of hope for Nathan's understanding blossomed within. A strong part of her believed Helena's speech about soul mates and believed, too, that he was her destiny.

"Listen to me," she muttered under her breath, then sniffed away threatening tears. "I've screwed this whole thing up. There's no way he's going to forgive me. Practically everything I've told him is a lie." She glanced in the rearview mirror and didn't recognize her own stare.

She had become a different woman since Travis Edwards stormed into her life. The incredible thing was she was grateful—to both of them. And her aunt had been right as well. She needed to take a leap of faith.

She arrived at the hospital steeled with courage and a prepared speech cemented in her head. But her heart seemed to have dropped into the pit of her stomach.

"Carissa." Nathan's familiar voice thundered behind her.

She froze.

"I've been looking all over for you." He encircled her in his arms and planted a kiss on her cheek. "I thought you'd never get here," he said, leading her down the hallway.

"Where are we going? Aren't we going to the—"

"Didn't you get my messages?" He stopped and faced her.

Confused, she shook her head.

"He's awake."

Panic seized her. "What?"

"I know. I can hardly believe it!" In one grand swoop, he swung her around, then set her back down on weak knees. "Wait until you see him. The doctors are amazed at how well he's doing. He's talking and everything." He turned again and tugged at her arm.

Her mind reeled. "How? When?"

"Isn't it great?" He pulled her back into his arms in a fierce hug. "I got my second chance, just like you said. I owe so much to you," he whispered against her ear, then turned to lead her back down the hall.

A chill slithered down her spine. She was seconds from losing him. "Wait. There's something I have to tell you." She dug in her heels, trying again to stop him from dragging her into Travis Edwards's room.

"Can't it wait?" He laughed incredulously.

"No. This *definitely* can't wait."

He frowned. "What can't possibly wait?"

Carissa stared wide-eyed at him, unable to find her voice.

Nathan's brows furrowed and his frown deepened. "What is it?" When she didn't readily respond, he pulled her into his arms and laughed. "Come on. We can talk later. Wait until you see him. I've been talking his head off for the past hour."

With that, he managed to escort her the rest of the way to Travis's room, where she expected her life to end.

"Dad, look who I found roaming out in the hallway."

The moment Travis's and Carissa's gazes crashed, the room instantly layered with an explosive tension. And in that same instant, she knew the game was finally over.

Carissa swallowed the lump lodged in her throat and watched with dread as Travis Edwards's smiling disposition darkened ominously.

"What are you doing here?" His gaze shifted to Nathan, his distrust mirrored in his eyes. "What's going on? Why the hell did you bring her here?"

Carissa pulled out of Nathan's grasp. "Calm down, Mr. Edwards," she said, worried about another heart attack. "I can explain." She turned toward Nathan's questioning gaze.

"You have some nerve coming here," Travis continued to bark. "I'm sure I've disappointed you by not dying, Cartel."

"Cartel?" Nathan's eyes darted between her and his father. "I don't understand."

"Didn't she tell you? Hell, I wouldn't be surprised if she didn't. That woman will stop at nothing to get what she wants." Contempt dripped in his voice.

Carissa whirled on her heel. "Stop it. That's not true." To her horror, a tear slid from her eyes.

Travis lifted an inquisitive brow. "Excuse me if I speak from experience."

What could she say? She doubted Travis would believe some fairy tale about the power of love and how it had helped her change her ways. Hell, she hardly believed it herself.

"Carissa?"

She closed her eyes against the tremble in his voice—or rather the undeniable pain layering it. Slowly, she turned as a steady stream of tears flowed from her eyes. His figure blurred from her vision. "I swear I wanted to tell you the truth."

He stepped back and stared at her as if he'd never seen her.

Her heart tightened. "My real name is Carissa Cartel. I'm the president of Cartel Enterprises. I didn't tell you who I was because…I thought you would blame me for what happened to your father."

"If he doesn't, I sure as hell do," Travis's boisterous voice interrupted.

She bit her lip and forced herself to face the older man. "I don't blame you for hating me. And I don't expect you to believe a word I say—"

"Good. Save your breath and get out."

She nodded and wiped her tears. "I'm truly sorry, Mr. Edwards." She managed to meet his gaze again. "I don't think you'll ever know how much."

For the briefest of seconds, she swore the older man's dark gaze softened.

"Then everything was a lie between us?" Nathan assessed in a firm yet troubled voice.

His words pierced her heart. She didn't know how to convince him otherwise, so why bother? The ensuing silence condemned her.

"I think you should leave, Ms. Cartel," Travis suggested.

To her utter amazement, she saw sympathy pool around his eyes. She nodded and headed out the door. Blinded by tears, Carissa struggled to get down the hall.

Seconds later, Nathan jerked her around to face him. "You were behind this all along?" Fire simmered in his gaze and burned a hole through her.

She stepped back and mouthed the word *no*. The accusation rumbled in her head like a freight train, rendering her powerless against the field of guilt it left in its wake.

He matched her movement, bearing down on her as if preparing to attack. "I should give you a taste of your own medicine. Maybe you'd like it if I stripped you of everything—robbed you of your dignity, *Cartel*. You had me running all over town on a wild-goose chase. What kind of person are you?"

Backed against the wall, she shook her head vehemently, still unable to voice any protest.

His head lowered. His hot breath rushed against her face and weakened her knees.

"Did his company mean that much to you? Where in the hell did I fit into all of this?"

His anger broke her heart. He *had* stripped her—with his words and disgust. She'd never felt this vulnerable—this ashamed.

"It was only business. It's not personal," she managed to whisper. Tears of remorse crested and splashed over the rims of her eyes.

"It sure as hell doesn't feel like business. I'm beginning to think that you don't know the difference."

"I'm sorry that you feel that way. I don't expect either of you to believe me. But I never meant for any of this to happen."

"How in the hell am I supposed to believe you?"

"I don't know," she said, shaking her head. Her body quaked with heart-wrenching sobs. When he moved away from her, it took everything she had not to reach for him.

"The game is over, Cartel." His voice dripped with disgust. "You stay away from me and my father."

Chapter 28

Carissa remained in bed for three days with a box of Kleenex. She'd refused to eat and had slept very little. *Why didn't I just tell him the truth?* The question swirled endlessly in her mind, accelerating her tears.

She'd lost everything. Nothing mattered anymore.

She clutched her pillow and buried her face in its softness. At any moment, she feared the growing ache within her would destroy her. The pain was the worst part, she concluded.

A soft knock sounded at the door, seconds before Helena poked her head through. "Good. You're up." She eased inside, carrying a tray. "I brought you some soup. And don't worry, the kitchen is still intact."

Carissa wiped her tears with the back of her hand. "I'm not hungry."

"You've got to eat something." Helena ignored her protest and sat the tray on the bed, then helped her try to sit up. "Oh, sweetheart. You look awful." She brushed her niece's unruly hair from her face to see the tracks of Carissa's tears. "Oh, baby. I'm so sorry that you're going through this."

"Yeah, right." Carissa shrugged from her aunt's touch. "Weren't you the one pushing for me to discover love?"

"But I never wanted you to end up with a broken heart. That's a pain I wouldn't wish on anyone."

"But it's a part of the deal, right?"

Helena sat on the edge of the bed. "Sometimes. I guess I would know that more than anyone."

"How do you do it?" Carissa's blurry gaze centered on her. "How do you get past the pain?"

"I know this is a cliché, but time really does heal all wounds."

"That's what you said about my father's death."

Helena lowered his gaze. "Some pain takes longer than others." She was silent for a moment before she looked up again. "But you can't give up on love, sweetie. There is such a thing as a soul mate. I still believe that."

"I don't see how you do it," Carissa responded honestly. "When this is all over, I can't imagine risking my heart again. It just hurts too damn much."

"I hope you're wrong," Helena said, finding her niece's gaze again. "I think you have so much to offer.

You're not as bad as you think you are. In the time that you spent with Nathan, I think you learned not to hate yourself so much. You let go of your guilt. You let your hair down and gave everyone a glimpse of the beautiful woman you are."

"And in the end, I lost the man I loved."

"Are you sure?"

Carissa moved the tray and stood from the bed. "If I've learned anything about Nathan, it's how much he treasures honesty. That's what's so terrible. I knew that and still…"

"You're not going to achieve anything by remaining cooped up in your bedroom and beating yourself up."

"Don't you think I deserve it?" Carissa snapped.

"No. I don't." Helena jumped to her feet. "You're selling yourself short and maybe even selling Nathan short. Tell him the truth. Sit him down and just explain why you didn't tell him who you were. There is such a thing as forgiveness."

Her aunt's heartfelt speech made sense. But the fear of more rejection warded off her hopes. "You weren't there. You didn't see how he looked at me. As if he didn't know me anymore." A sad laugh shook her small body. "But then again, how could he? I never told him who I was."

"He knows your heart. That's how he was able to fall in love with you. That's who he's still in love with."

Carissa turned, shaking her head. "You're a hopeless romantic, Auntie."

"I know. Now if I can just get you to follow in my footsteps."

* * *

Nathan lay on his couch and gazed into the darkness. How had he allowed this to happen again? Was he ever going to learn his lesson? He knew from experience that time healed all wounds, but he had a feeling he would never get over Carissa Cartel.

He could hear George as he trotted over and lay next to the couch. "I guess it's just you and me, kid." He reached down and caressed his soft coat.

Suddenly the living-room light clicked on and Gina entered.

"You're really starting to worry me, Nate."

Groaning, he sat up to make room for her on the couch. "Don't. I'm a big boy. I can take care of myself."

She slapped his bare back hard. "Don't get sassy with me. I know you and I know that you're hurting. But it seems to be that you won't be able to get past this until you at least go over and talk to her."

"Why? So she can tell me another lie? Gina, when I think about how stupid I must have looked to her, I just want to throw something."

"Look, I don't know the girl, but I have a feeling that there is more to this story than what meets the eye."

Nathan shook his head. "I appreciate what you're trying to do, but there's no point to this. You know how I feel about honesty. How can I build a relationship with someone I can't trust?"

Gina placed her hand against his cheek. "That's just it. I think that you *do* trust her." She held up a hand before he could interrupt. "I understand that you're disappointed. But after listening to you for the past couple of weeks, I have no doubts that you do trust her. Your heart trusts her. Just think about it."

"I still don't know, Gina. I don't think that I can forgive her." He expelled a long breath and shook his head. "I just can't stop feeling like a complete fool. You should have seen how I chased after her, fawning like some lovesick teenager. That's the worst thing. How can I forgive that?"

Gina lowered her head to avoid seeing the pain in his eyes. "I don't know. But can I ask you something?"

"Of course."

"What would you have said if she'd told you the truth?"

Nathan pulled himself up from the couch and paced in front of her. "Nothing. When we met, I had no idea what part Cartel played in my father's heart attack."

"Where were you when you did find out?"

He shrugged. "Nowhere. She'd refused my advances and pretty much stopped coming to the hospital."

Gina stood. "Don't you see? She was trying to protect you."

"Or she was trying to cover up her sins. No. I'm right about her," he declared with conviction. "She's lived up to the myth. She'll stop at nothing to get what she wants."

"And she's done all this to acquire Edwards Electronics?"

"Apparently."

Gina shook her head. "I don't buy it, Nate. Your father's company isn't even in the same league as Cartel Enterprises. It doesn't make sense that she would go through so much trouble just to acquire it."

"Look, I don't know much about corporate America. But I can't think of any other reason for her deceiving me like she did. You weren't here, so you can't possibly understand."

"Maybe you're right," Gina agreed. "Anyway, George and I are heading back to Miami in the morning. Do you know when you're coming home?"

"Soon. Travis should be out of the hospital soon. After that, it's business as usual."

"All right. I'm off to bed." She turned to leave, then stopped to face him again. "Look, you're never going to learn the truth by chasing speculation. Take my advice and go talk to her."

When Nathan lowered his head and didn't respond, she gave up. "Good night, guys." She reached down and scratched behind George's ears and went off to bed.

Colin Hunter spent the past three days watching his stepson's heartbreak slowly destroy him. And he was well aware that he was responsible. Yet he knew a confession would dissolve their relationship.

Maybe if he waited, Nathan would forget about Carissa Cartel and move on with his life. He shook his head. Who was he kidding? It was a matter of time before Travis told Nathan that Hunter worked for Cartel Enterprises. In fact, he was surprised that neither Travis nor Carissa had said anything.

Colin swiveled his chair around to stare out at the skyline of Atlanta. Even Cartel hadn't been in the office, which was out of character for a workaholic.

"You've really outdone yourself, old boy." He shook his head, wishing there were an easier route to undo the damage he'd done. But he wasn't going to get off that easy.

For years, he'd blamed Travis for his broken heart. Now he understood with perfect clarity that he needed to own up to his sins. And it all started when he fell in love with Valerie Edwards. He didn't mean to, it was just something that happened.

Colin stood from the chair and paced in front of the window as he remembered the past. While Travis was away in Vietnam, he'd believed it was his duty to look after Val, but the more he was around her, the more he loved her.

In reality, he knew she came to him out of loneliness and he took advantage of the situation. However, he wasn't prepared for Travis's return. Val made it clear that she was still in love with her husband and didn't want their affair to come to light. Colin had other plans.

He couldn't give her up that easily, and he was more than willing to sacrifice his relationship with his best friend for the love of his wife…

Chicago, 1972

"What the hell is going on here?" Travis's heated gaze darted from Val to Colin.

Neither spoke.

Travis took a threatening step toward his once-trusted friend, his hands clenched at his sides. "I asked you a question."

Colin watched helplessly as a wall of pain descended on his friend. How could he explain what had happened? How do you explain betrayal?

"You son of a bitch!" Travis flew toward him.

Before Colin could react, his head snapped back when Travis's steel fist landed across his jaw. The taste of blood seeped into his mouth. He tried to regain his bearing, but another punch jerked his head in the opposite direction.

Val's screams rang in his ears as he tried to hang on to consciousness. But something within him prevented him from fighting back. Somewhere in the back of his mind, he was convinced that he deserved it.

Colin wasn't too worried about Travis attacking Val. He knew that he would never lay a hand on her.

Hours later, Colin woke with a cold compress pressed to his forehead and with Val sobbing softly beside him.

"What happened?" he asked.

The question deepened her sobs. "He's gone."

A swell of relief washed over him. Lord knew he wasn't ready for round two of his beating. "I'm sure when he calms down, we can try to talk to him."

When she shook her head, he placed a reassuring hand against her shoulder. "I'm sorry. This is all my fault. I'll make him understand that I'm to blame in all of this. I'll leave town if I have to."

She looked at him then. "You don't understand. I know my husband. He's never going to forgive us and he's never coming back."

Colin closed his eyes from the pain of the past. He was responsible for Nathan's pain, and for nearly thirty years he'd kept the truth from him. But now he couldn't do it any longer. After Travis and Val's divorce, he stuck around, hoping against hope she'd learn to love him.

But she never did. She loved Travis until the day she died and that knowledge drove him to seek revenge. And he got his chance when Edwards Electronics experienced financial trouble. It all seemed so simple. He didn't expect the heart attack or any of the other ensuing medical problems. And the last thing he expected was for Nathan to come running to a man he confessed to hating for most of his life. But that's when everything got complicated.

If Nathan learned the truth, would he forgive him, or would he cut him out of his life as well? The thought scared him. But it was time to end the madness. Determined, Colin left his office and headed to Northside Hospital. It was time to talk to Travis and Nathan.

Chapter 29

Colin's heart hammered in his chest as he walked down the halls of Northside Hospital. The stakes were high. Not only was he laying his pride on the line and subjecting himself to humiliation in front of Travis, but he was sure that he was about to lose the most important person in his life: his son.

He arrived in front of Travis's private room all too soon, and his perfectly prepared speech seemed to have evaporated in his head. Yet he couldn't turn back now. He could never turn back.

His hands trembled as he pressed against the door and entered. He didn't get far into the room before Travis's murderous glare stopped him dead in his tracks.

"I see the doctors were wrong." Travis's gruff voice

boomed in the room. "I did die. And since you're here, this must be hell."

Despite the circumstances, Travis' sarcasm won a slight smile from Colin. "I see you haven't lost your wonderful sense of humor."

"Humph." Travis glanced away. "So to what do I owe this displeasure? Are you here looking for *my* son?"

Colin's smile flatlined. "I was hoping that he'd be here."

"Well, you just missed him. So you can leave now."

He wanted to leave. Hell, he wanted to run. "Actually, I wanted to talk to you, too." When Travis didn't respond, Colin's brows dipped in confusion. "I have to admit, I'm surprised you're not hollering and screaming at me."

Travis's cold stare shifted back to him. "You'd like that, wouldn't you? Is that why you came here, hoping that I'd have another attack?"

"No. I came to try to set things right between us."

"You're a little late, aren't you?"

"Yes, but better late than never."

"Is that up for debate?" Travis expelled a long, frustrated sigh. "Smokey, I'm really not up for this. I'm old and I'm tired—too tired to be angry anymore."

Colin slid his hands into his pockets and moved closer. "I only need a few minutes of your time."

Travis groaned.

"Just five minutes, then I'll leave." When Colin's

gaze met his old friend's, he feared he would be turned away, so he added, "Please."

"Five minutes, then I want you out of here."

Now that he had the time, his apology jumbled in his head. "Believe it or not, I don't know where to begin."

"How about starting with why," Travis suggested. "Actually, it's the only thing I really want to know."

"You know why. You remember what it was like just to be around Val…her smile, her laughter. She had a way of getting into your blood."

Travis grunted. "Those were the reasons that I married her. Little did I know that I had to keep my eye on my best friend." His hands clenched. "Damn it. You were my best friend. I trusted you. I trusted Val. Then you kept me from my son. He believes that I deserted him. In all those years, he only received one letter and it was when he was in college."

"I had no right to keep your letters from him." Colin's heart pounded in his ears. "What did you tell him?"

Travis laughed. "Afraid that I ratted you out?" He shook his head. "At last we discover the real reason you came. Well, you can rest easy. Your secret is safe with me."

Colin's mouth fell open in shock.

"Don't look so surprised. It's obvious to me the boy's crazy about you. I don't see any reason to upset him any further than he already is."

"You're referring to him and Cartel's breakup?"

Travis leaned back against his pillows. "I had no idea that there was something between them. I was just so damn angry when I saw her that I let my anger get the best of me. The next thing I knew…" He closed his eyes. "She loves him. It was written all over her face."

Colin nodded. "We need to figure out some way to get those two together again."

"We?"

"Look. I'm not asking that we try to be friends again. But neither of us wants to hurt Nathan. And I can tell you that I've never seen him as happy as he was with Carissa."

"Carissa." Travis laughed. "I never dreamed of calling Cartel by her first name, let alone that I'd be sitting here trying to figure out a way to get her into the family—dysfunctional as it may be."

"After I leave here, I'm going over to talk to him. You may not think that it's necessary to bring up the past, but I have to come clean with Nathan for what I've done. I'm praying he'll forgive me, and if he can forgive you and me, surely he can forgive the love of his life."

"Doesn't sound like much of a plan. While you're out committing suicide, I'll be here coming up with plan B."

Nathan turned his back to Smokey and braced his hands against the wall as every muscle in his body tensed. "How could you have done this to me? How could you have remained silent about what really happened?"

"I'm not proud of what I've done. But I'm trying to fix this mess I've caused. I just hope you can find it in your heart to forgive me." Smokey's voice trembled as he spoke.

Nathan closed his eyes against another wave of pain, pain that was caused by a lifetime of betrayal and deceit. "You're asking a lot from me," he whispered.

"I know. I'm not sure if I would forgive me either if I were you."

Nathan turned and faced him. "How am I supposed to trust you—hell, trust anyone again? Everyone I have ever allowed to get close to me has betrayed me."

Smokey's gaze fell, but not before Nathan saw the raw pain that reflected in them.

"Are you saying that you are able to forgive Travis but not me?"

The question packed one hell of a punch and made Nathan erupt with guilt. "Damn." How was it that he was the one that felt guilty now? He wasn't the one who'd lied for nearly thirty years. "Why are you telling me all this now? Were you afraid that Travis would rat you out?"

Smokey rammed his hands into his pockets while his lowered gaze condemned him.

"I don't believe this," Nathan said, shaking his head. "It's like I'm living a nightmare. In one hour you've told me that my father walked out on me and my mother because he caught you two in an affair.

Then you tell me that he'd actually written to me several times when I was growing up, but you never said a word, and to top if off, you seized an opportunity to take over the man's company by convincing your employer to do a hostile takeover. Not to mention this is the same infamous employer who you knew I've been looking for for the past month and was actually the woman I was falling in love with. Did I leave anything out?"

"No," Smokey said as his shoulders sagged. "I know that I've made a mess of everything. God knows your mother reminded me of that every time she took a drink."

"Don't you *dare* pin this on my mother. By your own confession, you said that you took advantage of her loneliness. What went through your mind when you decided to betray your best friend? Isn't that what you guys were before all of this? Did it ever occur to you that she died of a broken heart?" Nathan said, defending his mother. "Do you realize that you single-handedly destroyed my family?"

Smokey stepped forward as his eyes glossed with tears, but before he could speak, Nathan stepped back.

They stared at each other through a painful silence, seemingly trapped in a stalemate.

"You have to know that I never meant to hurt you."

"But you did."

"And I'm sorry for it. I'm sorry for a lot of things. I wish like hell that I could turn back the hands of time. I would do so many things differently."

Nathan snorted in disgust and turned away. He walked into the kitchen and got himself a beer, then waited until he took a long swig before he said anything. "So what do you want from me? You want me to say it's okay—it's in the past? Or maybe I should say that I never want to see you again. You might not have heard, but I'm in the process of simplifying my life. This year alone I've gotten rid of two fiancées."

"Two?"

This time, Nathan's gaze fell. He took another swig of beer. "Can you believe it? I'd actually believed that I'd found my soul mate—a woman I'd looked forward to waking up next to for the rest of my life. She was someone who understood and had experienced the same kind of pain. She was also a woman I was just happy as hell to be around." His voice dipped and he struggled to control his mounting despair.

"None of that has changed," Smokey pointed out. "She's still the same woman you fell in love with. I mean, given the circumstances, I can see why she'd keep her identity from you."

"Now why doesn't that surprise me?"

"Okay." Smokey took the blow with an uplifted chin. "I deserved that. But when you're through casting judgment on us mere mortals, your highness, you just might wake up in time to go catch your soul mate before it's too late." Smokey turned and headed toward the door.

"What the hell does that mean?" Nathan shouted out to him.

"Just what I said. Cartel may be my employer, and maybe I've never gotten the chance to know her on the level you have. But I know enough to know that in the short time that you two have known each other, you were the happiest you have ever been. And since you broke up with her, it's been the worst I've ever seen you. That has to tell you something."

For the first time that night, Nathan's hard features softened.

"I can understand if you never want to speak to me again. I admittedly deserve your anger. But I'm not so sure that Cartel does."

"Stop calling her by her last name," Nathan mumbled irritably.

"Okay. I don't think that Carissa deserves your anger. Have you really thought about how you would have reacted if she'd told her real name? Didn't you say that when you first met her you were rude?"

You must be my father's latest conquest. Nathan cringed as his first words floated back into his consciousness.

"How was she supposed to tell you that she felt responsible for Travis's heart attack? And if your father had died, her guilt would have destroyed her. Didn't you tell me that she already feels responsible for her own father's death?"

Nathan nodded as he digested everything.

"You know, if I were her," Smokey went on, "I'd try to avoid you. But wait a minute, she tried that, didn't she?"

Nathan's frown deepened. She had refused to have dinner with him, then stopped coming to the hospital. He was the one who had pursued her, refusing to take no for an answer. He looked to his stepfather. "Did she send you over here to present her case?"

"Now you don't really believe that, do you?"

He shook his head and set his beer down on the counter. Everything Smokey had said made perfect sense. "You know there were a few times I remember her trying to tell me something, but I always told her she could tell me later. I just never dreamed that she was simply trying to tell me her name."

"But what about all the stuff that she did do? What happened to all those things that had you walking on cloud nine and had you willing to jump into the relationship with blinders on?"

Nathan clamped his mouth shut.

"Didn't she help you bury the past and had even preached about second chances with Travis? That hardly sounds like a crime to me. Hell, when all this is over I hope to enlist her help to get you to forgive me, because despite what you may think, I'm truly sorry…for everything. I love you, son." Smokey opened the front door.

"Pop?"

Smokey stopped, his heart swelling with hope. He turned to face his son.

There were tears in Nathan's eyes as the corners of his mouth lifted. "I don't want you to go."

Chapter 30

One month later

Sitting on top of the world—what a joke.

Carissa's dispirited gaze roamed across the Atlanta cityscape while remorse settled in her chest. *I can't do this anymore,* she said to herself. *I can't go back to business as usual.*

With each passing day, she thought more about dropping everything and just going, but she didn't know where. She just couldn't keep masquerading as the cold and ruthless C. J. Cartel anymore.

She turned from the window and walked to her desk, where she picked up Colin Hunter's letter of resignation. "It's just as well," she said to her aunt, who sat in the chair across from her desk. "It saved me the trouble of firing him. No doubt he's been able to walk away from this whole fiasco unscathed."

"Don't you worry about him. I firmly believe that what goes around comes around. A man like that will get his due. You can trust me on that one."

Carissa exhaled and shook her head. "I know that this may sound strange, but I actually feel sorry for him."

"You're right. That does sound strange. If I weren't a lady I'd pound the weasel into the ground myself."

Carissa laughed at the image. "Now why don't I have any trouble believing that? But let's face it. Everything he'd done, he did for love—or what he thought was love. He loved Nathan's mother and, I guess, did whatever he could to keep her."

"There *is* such a thing as crossing the line, Risa. And look at the mess he's made. Sometimes you have to learn to walk away from love."

"Tell me something that I don't know." Carissa lowered her head. "Maybe once I leave here, I can begin making some sense out of my life."

"You're doing the right thing by stepping down as president and CEO," Helena said. "You hated working here."

"More like I hated what I'd become. But there were some good things about the job. I'm proud of a lot of my accomplishments here."

"You'll still be a member of the board."

"I know. It just feels strange, that's all. Then again, it's exciting. I think I'll take up dancing again, maybe teach in a small studio somewhere."

"That sounds nice. Summer is just around the corner. You know that you're more than welcome to come with me to Costa Rica. Then after that I think I'll jet off to Spain."

Carissa considered it. Maybe it was time for her to start taking chances, to do exciting things. "I've always wanted to go to Morocco. You think we can add it to the list?"

Helena's face brightened. "Of course we can." She clapped her hands together. "This is going to be great. Just picture it, you and me traveling around the world without a care. There will be fun, lots of dancing and plenty of men. Which brings me to another philosophy of mine. 'Nothing helps you get over this man like the next man.'"

"You're impossible." Carissa laughed. She leaned back in her chair and reviewed her options. "So when do we leave?"

Liz buzzed in over the intercom. "Ms. Cartel, you have a visitor."

Carissa frowned. "I asked for all my appointments to be rescheduled."

"Yes, ma'am. This gentleman wasn't on your calendar, but he's insisting on seeing you." Liz's voice lowered to a whisper. "I think you really want to take this visitor, Risa."

"All right, send him in." Carissa straightened in her

chair and tried to get into character. "Maybe we should talk about this later, Auntie."

Helena stood. "Okay. I'm going to call my travel agent. We're going to have so much fun." She headed out just when Liz knocked, then opened the door.

Nothing could have prepared Carissa for who waltzed inside.

Travis Edwards met her startled gaze with a cool, satisfied smile. "Good morning, Ms. Cartel. I hope I'm not inconveniencing you."

"Holy smoke," Helena said, staring at Edwards. "You're an older replica of—"

"Aunt Helena, I'll see you tonight," Carissa said, cutting her off.

Helena turned with a questioning look.

"It's okay."

Liz also gave an apologetic look, then eased out of the room with Helena following close behind.

Carissa stood, not sure of what to say, then sat down again. He looked good, damn good. His domineering presence filled the room, while his striking resemblance to Nathan tore her apart.

"Please, don't get up," Travis said, moving toward her desk.

"I didn't know you were out of the hospital."

"Are you disappointed?"

"Of course not. But I have to admit I'm a little surprised to see you here." She crossed her arms, unable to quell her guilt. The last thing she wanted to do was beg this man for forgiveness…again. "Don't tell me you came all this way to finish me off?"

He held up his hand as a sign of surrender. "No need to get defensive. I guess someone should have called and informed my fiancée of my release."

Embarrassment heated Carissa's face. "I was afraid that you'd hear about that."

"I heard a lot of things."

"I was afraid of that, too," she said despondently.

He shrugged. "Actually, I was touched."

She met his gaze. "Mr. Edwards, I don't know how to say this. But I'm terribly sorry about what happened. It was never my intention to wish you any harm, nor did I have some hidden agenda to destroy your company. You've got to believe that."

"I know."

"I wish there was something I could—"

She stopped. "What do you mean, you 'know'?"

He sat in the vacant chair in front of her desk. "Let's just say I had a very interesting talk with your vice president."

"Ex-vice president," she corrected, then asked, perplexed, "Colin told you of his involvement?"

"That and a whole lot more." Travis folded his hands. "I know this may sound strange, but it's starting to look like this hostile takeover was the best thing that has ever happened to me."

"You must be joking."

He shook his head and smiled. "The truth is, Ms. Cartel, I came here to thank you."

"Thank me? For what?"

"For giving me my son back. Nathan said that it was you who convinced him to stay and try to bury our past. I thought I'd never see this day. I have you to thank for it."

Carissa stood and moved toward the window. "I'm happy you two will have a second chance to become a real father and son. I wish I'd been so lucky." She swallowed the lump lodged in her throat. "But I am glad that you're here. I need to talk to you about Edwards Electronics." She straightened her shoulders, then turned to face him. "I decided to revert control back over to you."

Surprise registered in his eyes. "You're giving me back my company?"

"It's not exactly a wise business move for me, but it's definitely the right thing to do."

He stared at her for a long time, then looked down at his braided fingers. "I'm not going to pretend that I understand you, Cartel."

She shook her head and laughed sadly. "How could you? I don't understand myself." She drew in a deep breath. "But you can start by calling me Carissa."

His smile broadened as he stood. "Very well, Carissa. Thank you, but no thank you."

"What?"

"Well, I've thought about it and I think it's time for me to slow down—take time out and smell the roses as they say. I'm going to enjoy some time with my son. We have a lot of years to make up."

Tears stung the back of her eyes. "That sounds great. I'm happy for you."

"Well, I better get going. Again, I want to thank you."

"You're welcome, I think." She nodded, lowering her gaze, and she struggled on whether she should ask about Nathan. No, she decided. It was over. The sooner she accepted that, the better off she'd be.

"Could you tell him I'm sorry," she whispered. "I know what I did hurt him and I just want him to know how sorry I am."

When she looked up, Travis smiled. "I tell you what—I'll let you tell him." He opened the door and Nathan entered.

Carissa's heart squeezed at the sight of him. She couldn't breathe, she couldn't think, and, God, he looked good. Dressed in black, he appeared more handsome than she remembered.

"I'm going to leave you two alone," Travis said, then eased out of the office.

Nathan and Carissa stood facing each other. A strange and powerful electrical current streamed between them.

"So this is what the inside of your office looks like." He glanced around, nodding.

She nodded. "I guess I deserved that."

"I didn't mean it the way it sounded," he apologized.

Another awkward silence lapsed between them before he tried again. "So how have you been?"

"Miserable," she answered honestly. "And you?"

"Pretty much the same."

"Now that you're here, I don't know where to begin." Her eyes moistened as her voice softened into a whisper. "There's so much I have to tell you—things I need to explain."

He crossed his arms and studied her. "Sounds like another all-nighter."

Nervous, she shifted her weight under his scrutiny. "Please don't do that."

"Do what?"

"Stare at me like that. It makes me feel like a convict on death row. This is hard enough."

Nathan laughed.

Her eyes narrowed. "Do you find this funny?"

"Only because you're trying to pick a fight with me in order to ease your guilt. Let's face it, saying you're sorry or apologizing has never been your best suit."

"I did apologize, remember?"

"Good point. What can I say? I was hurt. But then I realized that it wasn't your name that I fell in love with. It's important that I know things about you. That way, I know that the *person* I fell in love with is real."

Carissa's eyes widened in surprise. "You love me?"

"How could I not?" He walked toward her. "I spent a lot of time going over in my head all the things that I know and love about you. Like, I love that you have a quick temper. And that at times you appear so child-like, then the next moment you're this spitfire. I love your compassion, and I love the fact that you're here right now." He now stood just inches in front of her. "I've missed you, Risa."

She neither knew how she remained standing nor whether she could trust her hearing. "What happened between you and Smokey?"

He drew in a deep breath. "We fought, we cried, and we've made up. Despite everything that has happened, I still love him. Nothing is going to change that. It's going to take time for all the wounds to heal, but they will heal. I think it will be a while before he and Travis bury the hatchet. But you never know."

"It would be nice if they did," she conceded.

"After talking with Smokey, I understand more why you lied to me. To tell you the truth, I'm not so sure I wouldn't have done the same thing myself."

"No, you wouldn't have, Honest Abe. Besides, you weren't too forgiving at the hospital."

"Okay, maybe not. But aren't I allowed to make mistakes, too?" He pulled her into his arms. "I've missed you so much. Every time I turn around, I see your face and smell your perfume. I love you so much. I don't want to live another day without you in my life."

"Despite my name?"

"Carnes, Cartel—it doesn't matter. But I'm actually leaning more toward Edwards. Carissa Edwards. I love the way that sounds."

Her arms flew around his neck as their lips met in a passionate kiss. When they withdrew, Carissa snuggled within the crook of his neck. "I love you, too," she whispered. "And I hope you know what you're getting yourself into because I'm never letting you go again."

His arms tightened around her. "I guess this means that life is full of second chances." Nathan's head descended to seal their love with a kiss, but the moment his lips landed on hers, his body craved something more. Suddenly, their hands were tearing at each other's clothes.

"I've been dreaming of this moment for too long," Nathan said huskily. His eyes drifted closed at the exotic feel of her tongue dancing across his lower earlobe. At the same time, his hands managed to free her breasts from their lacy confinement.

"Oh, I've missed you so much," she whispered, then leaned her head back as his lips caressed her neck.

Their clothes fell in pieces and formed a trail heading to the couch. There was no way they were going to wait until they were home.

Helena, Travis, Smokey and Liz stood from having their ears pressed against the door. Each wore a wide smile of satisfaction.

"I think I'm going to cry," Helena said, trying to retrieve a tissue from her purse.

Travis handed her his handkerchief. "I can't believe we've pulled it off," he said to Smokey.

"I'm no fortune teller, but I'd say we'll be planning a wedding here soon."

"Now, I know I'm going to cry." Liz wiped at her eyes and was rewarded with Smokey's handkerchief.

* * *

Much later, Carissa and Nathan lay spent in each other's arms and wore smiles of satisfaction. Carissa loved the way their different skin tones complemented each other. This was the man she wanted to share the rest of her life with, and he was what completed her.

"There you go thinking again." Nathan lifted her chin to claim another kiss. "Should I dare ask what steals your attention from me?"

"Actually, I was thinking about you—or shall I say us."

"You're not having second thoughts, are you?" His eyes darkened with concern.

"Never."

"Good." Their lips met again before Nathan grew serious. "Now that we are going to spend the rest of our lives together, I think it's time we have a little talk about honesty and communication."

"I was afraid of that." She bit her lower lip.

He laughed. "It's very important to me that you never feel that there's something you can't tell me. No matter how much you think it may upset me, I want you to come to me. Agreed?"

"Agreed." She stole another kiss, then slid her arms around her future husband. "I love you, Nathan Edwards."

"I love you, too, Risa."

Chapter 31

Six months later

Nathan carried Carissa across the threshold and into their honeymoon suite. Their lips remained locked in a passionate kiss as he continued to carry her blindly to the king-size bed.

When their lips finally parted, it was only long enough for him to whisper, "I love you, Mrs. Edwards."

"Not half as much as I love you."

Nathan slid next to her and immediately fumbled with the buttons on her blouse.

Greedily, she tugged at his clothes, but couldn't

stop herself from laughing at their sense of urgency. They'd chosen to remain celibate since they'd announced their engagement. Both had agreed that the wait would enhance their wedding night and give them something to look forward to.

So far they had been right.

Nathan's brows arched in surprise at the discovery of her red lace teddy. "You really know how to melt a man's heart," he complimented with a cocky grin.

Carissa ran her hand down the corded muscles of his chest. "You're not doing such a bad job with me yourself." She winked.

"Has anyone ever told you that you're too much of a tease, Mrs. Edwards?" His head descended to capture a tan nipple between his teeth.

Carissa's head lolled back as a moan escaped her lips. Her body arched as her mind's passion-filled haze thickened. How was it that he knew her body so well? How was it that she came alive with just the simple touch of his hand?

"You're mine," he whispered huskily, just as his fingers invaded the dewy folds of her womanhood. Waves of ecstasy rippled throughout her body. It was as though she were suspended through time and space.

Tears of joy slid from her eyes as he entered her and filled the void in her life. As their bodies found their own tempo, Carissa's moans of pleasure reverberated throughout the room and sounded like sweet music in his ears.

Throughout the night, the couple experimented with exotic oils, candle wax, feathers and Carissa's favorite…blindfolds.

"I wish it will always be this way between us," Carissa said, snuggling closer to her exhausted husband.

"It will be. When we go back to Miami, I have a nice little surprise for you."

"What is it?"

"I can't tell you. It's a surprise."

She sat up. "You expect me to wait after our three-week honeymoon to find out what the surprise is?"

"Yep." He rolled over and pretended to go to sleep.

"I don't think so." She shook him and became frustrated when he started to snore. "You're not asleep, Nathan. Tell me what it is?"

His snoring grew louder.

Carissa playfully pounded his back. "Wake up, you brute. And tell me what the surprise is."

With lightning speed, Nathan turned over and pinned his wife to the bed. "I'm the brute? Aren't *you* the one beating *me* up?"

Carissa laughed as she tried to break free from his iron grip.

"You want to know what the secret is?"

She stopped struggling and nodded.

"I found this nice little studio, not too far from our place, that I thought would be perfect for you to teach dance."

Carissa's eyes grew wide. "Really?"

He released her and was immediately rewarded with a fierce hug.

"I can't believe it," she cried excitedly. "My own dance studio?"

"You haven't even seen the place yet."

"It doesn't matter." She pulled back to stare at him. "I know that I'm going to love it. Just as I know that I'm always going to love you."

"That's good to know because I'm always going to love you, too."

Epilogue

Dear Aunt Helena,

Greetings from Morocco. We're having a wonderful time here. If you ever get the chance, you should add this wonderful place to your travel schedule. I hope you enjoy the enclosed pictures. I took them myself.

By the way, Nathan finally told me you guys' secret. I can't believe you actually crashed his bachelor party. What on earth are we going to do with you?

Wasn't it great to see Travis and Smokey serving as groomsmen at the wedding? Who knows, maybe there's still a chance for them to bury the hatchet. Let's keep our fingers crossed.

Well, I have to go. I hope to see you soon,
Love,
Risa

Dear Risa,

Thanks for the pictures. Next time try to keep your finger out of the shots. I hope we'll soon hear the pitter-patter of little feet.

You'll never guess what has happened. I met this wonderful man in Las Vegas last week. His name is Charlie and he's a doctor. He's also ten years younger than me, but what the heck? Anyway, we had a blast, painting the town. And guess what—we eloped. (Lucky number seven.)

I can't wait until you meet him.

Love,

Helena

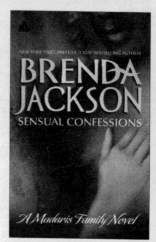

REQUEST YOUR FREE BOOKS!

2 FREE NOVELS
PLUS 2 FREE GIFTS!

KIMANI ROMANCE ™

Love's ultimate destination!

YES! Please send me 2 FREE Kimani™ Romance novels and my 2 FREE gifts (gifts are worth about $10). After receiving them, if I don't wish to receive any more books, I can return the shipping statement marked "cancel." If I don't cancel, I will receive 4 brand-new novels every month and be billed just $4.69 per book in the U.S. or $5.24 per book in Canada. That's a saving of over 20% off the cover price. It's quite a bargain! Shipping and handling is just 50¢ per book in the U.S. and 75¢ per book in Canada.* I understand that accepting the 2 free books and gifts places me under no obligation to buy anything. I can always return a shipment and cancel at any time. Even if I never buy another book from Kimani Press, the two free books and gifts are mine to keep forever.

168 XDN E4CA   368 XDN E4CM

Name _____ (PLEASE PRINT) _____

Address _____ Apt. # _____

City _____ State/Prov. _____ Zip/Postal Code _____

Signature (if under 18, a parent or guardian must sign)

Mail to The Reader Service:
IN U.S.A.: P.O. Box 1867, Buffalo, NY 14240-1867
IN CANADA: P.O. Box 609, Fort Erie, Ontario L2A 5X3

Not valid for current subscribers to Kimani Romance books.

Want to try two free books from another line?
Call 1-800-873-8635 or visit www.morefreebooks.com.

* Terms and prices subject to change without notice. Prices do not include applicable taxes. N.Y. residents add applicable sales tax. Canadian residents will be charged applicable provincial taxes and GST. Offer not valid in Quebec. This offer is limited to one order per household. All orders subject to approval. Credit or debit balances in a customer's account(s) may be offset by any other outstanding balance owed by or to the customer. Please allow 4 to 6 weeks for delivery. Offer available while quantities last.

Your Privacy: Kimani Press is committed to protecting your privacy. Our Privacy Policy is available online at www.eHarlequin.com or upon request from the Reader Service. From time to time we make our lists of customers available to reputable third parties who may have a product or service of interest to you. If you would prefer we not share your name and address, please check here. ☐

Help us get it right—We strive for accurate, respectful and relevant communications. To clarify or modify your communication preferences, visit us at www.ReaderService.com/consumerschoice.

KROM10